Also by Ron Schwab

Sioux Sunrise

Paint the Hills Red

Grit

Cut Nose

The Lockes

Last Will

Medicine Wheel

Hell's Fire

The Law Wranglers

Deal with the Devil

Mouth of Hell

The Last Hunt

Summer's Child

Adam's First Wife

Escape from El Gato

Peyote Spirits

The Coyote Saga

Night of the Coyote

Return of the Coyote

Twilight of the Coyote

Escape from El Gato

The Law Wranglers

Ron Schwab

Uplands Press

OMAHA, NEBRASKA

Uplands Press
1401 S 64th Avenue
Omaha, NE 68106
www.uplandspress.com

Ordering Information:
Quantity sales. Special discounts are available on quantity purchases by corporations, associations, and others. For details, contact the "Special Sales Department" at the address above.

Uplands Press / Ron Schwab -- 1st ed.

ISBN 978-1-943421-43-5

Escape from El Gato

The Law Wranglers

Chapter 1

A FLUFFY BLANKET OF rolling clouds blocked the light that would otherwise have sifted through the whispering pine and aspen this pitch-black night. The coals left by the campfire glowed intermittently when offered a breath of life by a gust of soft wind. The first of June had passed a week earlier, but, come nightfall, the mountains of northern New Mexico ignored the season and dropped a chill over the slopes that became downright unpleasant to non-furbearing occupants.

Tabitha Rivers fought back the urge to toss a few logs on the dying embers, crowding closer to the remnants of warmth as she sat in the eerie stillness across from her cousin, North Star. Her brother, Cal Rivers, had deserted his spot at the fire a half-hour earlier, admonishing them not to feed the flames before he disappeared into the woods. "Quiet," Cal had warned, pressing forefinger to lips.

Obviously, something was troubling Cal. A former Army scout with Colonel Ranald Slidell Mackenzie during the Red River War, he had scouted Comanche close-up, occasionally stealing into their villages undetected to spy out information. She was not about to challenge his concerns, not when he was sober—and he had been for ten days now.

Tabitha started when she looked up and saw a figure silently slipping out of the darkness and stepping to within a few paces behind North Star before halting. It was almost a ghostlike form, but as the phantom stood there, she could make out a man's penetrating eyes that stared directly at her. He held a rifle waist high and pointed at North Star's back. As her eyes adjusted, she made out a face that would not have been unpleasant but for the scowl. He was naked above the twisted rawhide belt that held a warclub and wore a breechcloth that dropped to his knees just above calf-high moccasins. A wide cloth band or kerchief covered most of his forehead. She did not think his attire was Navajo. If not, geography suggested Apache of one band or another.

"What is it?" North Star asked.

"Don't turn around. We have company." Her first instinct was to reach for her Henry rifle, but there was no chance she could grab the weapon, lever a cartridge into the breech, and squeeze the trigger before the stranger fired his own weapon. He seemed to be perusing her like a horse he wanted to steal or buy. Not for the first time, Tabitha was having second thoughts about this journey. She had left a note for her friend and lover, Oliver Wolf, in Santa Fe and impulsively embarked on a quest to the Navajo homeland to learn of her mother's ancestors and seek inspiration and knowledge for a book she hoped to write. Now this presumed Apache would determine whether her search was ended.

"Who is the guest?" North Star asked, speaking softly and calmly.

"I think he is Apache, and he has a rifle leveled at your back."

"I find neither thought comforting. The two together are near terrifying."

The visitor finally spoke. "Woman. Name?"

Tabitha was relieved to learn the Indian spoke a few fragments of English. She spoke none of the native languages, although she was semi-fluent in Spanish, thanks to her New Mexican upbringing and her sister-in-law and best friend, Jael Rivers, who had a rare affinity for languages and spoke at least five or six fluently.

She decided her nickname would be easier for the inquirer to pronounce, so she said, "Tabby. Who are you?"

His brow furrowed, and he seemed somewhat taken aback that she would ask his name. Evidently, she was expected to answer all the questions. "El Gato," he said.

El Gato. Spanish for "the cat." She had seen his name mentioned in a *Santa Fe Daily New Mexican* story. She had noted the name because of the translation. As she recalled, El Gato was a sub-chief of some sort of the Chiricahua Apaches Mimbres band, who had joined Victorio in leading many of their tribespeople from the San Carlos reservation a few years back. They had returned and departed the reservation several times since. The last she had read, Victorio was currently at San Carlos, but El Gato obviously had either not joined him there or jumped the reservation. His band was evidently at war with the whites again and, doubtless, the Mexicans south of the border. But what was he doing so far north? And, certainly, he would not be alone. What happened to Cal?

The Apache continued, "Ta-Bee come. No hurt. No kill man." He nudged the rifle barrel toward North Star's back. "Where yellow-hair man?"

Tabitha said, "The other man is scouting ahead. He is not here."

"Lie. Horse here."

"He left afoot."

"Ta-Bee mans?" El Gato held up two fingers. Was he asking if the men were her husbands?

"The tall man is my brother. This man is my cousin."

"No man?"

"My man is in Santa Fe." If she still had a man, she thought.

"Watch Ta-bee moons." He held up three fingers. Three days? "Come. Ta-Bee El Gato woman now. Come with me."

The determined look on El Gato's grim face told her that he was issuing an order, not an invitation. She was certain North Star would die if she disobeyed, and she likely would also. She scrambled to her feet, again eyeing her rifle and weighing whether she should risk a lunge for it. Sanity won out. She was clad in buckskin shirt and britches and moccasins, but they would not ward off the chill, so she picked up the wool blanket she had been sitting on and tugged it about her shoulders.

North Star said, "Tabby, do not go with him. It is better that we die here. They will—" He was cut off when the rifle butt struck the back of his skull.

"You said you would not harm him," Tabitha accused the Apache.

"Say no kill. Ta-Bee come."

She could see that North Star was breathing, and she had no other choice. She stepped around the fire's remnants toward El Gato, noting that he was a sinewy man about North Star's height, making him several inches under six feet, tall for the native peoples she had known. He reached out to clasp her arm when the rapid explosions of gunshots broke the night's eerie silence. At the sound, he whirled away, his attention now focused on the forest. Another series of shots sent Tabitha dashing for her Henry rifle, and she swept it up and levered a cartridge into the breech in a single fluid motion. She turned to fire, but the Apache had disappeared into the darkness, swiftly and silently as his namesake.

She knelt beside North Star, who was moaning and trying to lift his head. She rushed to her pup tent and grabbed an old shirt that had already been partially shredded for wound dressings. The injury was swollen but not bleeding seriously, which she knew was not necessarily a good thing, but he seemed to be regaining his sensibilities quickly enough.

"Where did he go?" North Star asked.

"He disappeared. There were gunshots, and they scared him off. That's all that kept him from dragging me away."

"But whose gunshots? And why?"

"I don't know. I hope they were Cal's and not somebody shooting at him. Can you handle your rifle yet?"

He grabbed his Winchester, which, like Tabitha, he had kept nearby. "Help me get to cover. I am too dizzy to make it on my own, but if I get set someplace, I can fire a rifle."

She started to help him up when she heard someone moving through the trees and brush in their direction from outside the camp perimeter. Tabitha raised her rifle just as the unmistakable outline of her brother's tall frame broke into the clearing. Standing four or five inches over six feet, Cal Rivers was an imposing figure. She let loose a sigh of relief.

"Cal, I heard the gunshots. I was worried about you."

"Nothing to worry about, Little Sis—not yet anyhow. I took down two Apache warriors, who wasn't inclined to talk. And then when I came back this way, I seen another running from the camp, but he was moving like a scared deer. No way I was going to catch up to him. I don't know how he slipped past me to get up here. I was afraid he got to you and North Star."

"He got to us. The lump on North Star's head is proof of it. And he was going to take me with him when the gunfire started and distracted him. Then he disappeared fast as a rabbit."

Cal said, "I've had my eye out for several days. I seen unshod hoofprints and moccasin tracks within a half mile of us at different times, but we're close to Navajo country, and I figured they was friendlies and wouldn't be causing no trouble. Far north for Apaches."

North Star said, "The gunfire? That was yours and not the Apaches'?"

"I thought I heard a horse nicker downslope and went to check it out. Come upon two warriors holding three horses. One caught sight of me and fired at me twice—lousy shot. I didn't give him no third chance. I took out the other before he could nock an arrow. Knew there was another because of the three mounts, so I headed back here quick as I could."

Tabitha asked, "What was it all about? Why did the other two stay behind? If they wanted to kill us, I would have thought all three would have moved in."

"I'd guess the one man just came up to scout the camp, and, when he saw the two of you sittin' here, he figured he would just go ahead and finish his job. Was you he come for."

"For me?"

"Looks like it."

"Why?"

"Little Sis, I'm guessing some buck was looking for a woman, maybe a wife. It seems you are the one they was stalking."

Tabitha shuddered at the thought. "He said his name was El Gato—"the cat." I have read of him. I think he is a sub-chief or influential warrior. Mimbres. He was with Victorio when they jumped the reservation at San Carlos a few years back."

"Ain't heard of him. Don't matter none. We got to break camp and get the hell out of here. Someplace, there's a bigger war party, and when this El Gato tells his friends about the two dead warriors, they're apt to come after us."

North Star said, "We should be no more than a long day's ride from the Diné homeland. Perhaps, we can find refuge there." Diné was the Navajo word for "The People" and was how the tribespeople referred to themselves, Tabitha had learned from her Aunt Dezba, North Star's mother, who was full-blood Navajo. North Star's deceased father had been Pueblo. Tabitha had entered the family by virtue of being the love child of Summer Webb and Levi Rivers. Summer, who died at Tabitha's birth, had been Dezba's half-sister as the result of a shared mother. This accounted for Tabitha's quarter-blood Navajo heritage, which had triggered the obsession for her current quest.

In an hour's time the party was ready to ride with an extra horse and two mules, one fur-packed, trailing behind the caravan. A few hours out, Cal Rivers disappeared into the woods again.

Chapter 2

EL GATO REACHED the main war party mid-morning, leading the two horses with their dead riders slung over the mounts' backs. The other warriors watched silently as he entered the camp. Several came forward to unbind their fallen comrades and remove the bodies from the horses.

Speaking his native Apache tongue, El Gato said, "Find a cave or ravine and cover their bodies with stones. Our journey is too far to take them with us. A yellow-haired white man killed Raven Wing and Lone Horse. He is the brother of the woman I have claimed."

El Gato dismounted, and one of the warriors took his calico stallion. His friend and trusted lieutenant, Moon Watcher, a short, sinewy man and, like El Gato, in his early thirties, approached. "You lost two fine warriors and did not return with the woman," Moon Watcher chided.

Only his childhood friend could scold him like this. There were none more loyal to El Gato, but Moon Watcher never hesitated to speak his mind. "I entered the camp and was prepared to take the warrior woman with me when gunfire broke out. The brother had attacked Raven Wing and Lone Horse, who were waiting for me while I scouted the camp. I knew the brother's horse was in the remuda, but I did not see him near the camp. I thought he was afoot scouting ahead on the trail to the Navajo. The woman also said this, and I foolishly believed her."

"But, instead, he was stalking our brothers. Your obsession with this woman is clouding your judgment."

Moon Watcher's observation stung, but he knew his friend was right. Ever since he had watched her bathing naked in the stream, he had not been able to erase the woman from his memory. He would have captured her that day, but he had been alone and the yellow-hair and the Navajo she called cousin had been nearby and would have heard any scream or struggle. Two on a single horse would have been ridden down. And she would not have been taken willingly. He had been following for several days at that time, observing her feisty nature, her proficiency with a rifle when she brought down a buck, and the authority with which she conducted herself. There was no doubt that she was the encampment's chief, her status far different than that of any woman in an Apache village. She had bewitched him before he saw her bathing. That had only swept the fire out of control. She was like a wild horse waiting to be broken. And, yes, he would break her.

El Gato said, "The war party must go to the mountain stronghold in Mexico, where we left our women and children. Take the Navajo captives there. We can decide later which we will sell as slaves to the Mexicans and whether some are suitable as wives or worthy of becoming Mimbres. The two women appear strong and likely breeders. The older one has a son of eleven or twelve summers who might grow into an Apache warrior with proper teaching, older than I would like, but he has Apache spirit. The younger woman has a pretty face but has the shape of a skinny boy. I would sell her to the Mexicans if no warrior claims her. The two girl children could be sold with this woman. They should be nearing twelve summers, and I am told there are some Mexican and American men who seek such children to share their robes. They should bring high prices."

"I still say you should return with the war party."

"If I cannot capture this woman within ten suns, I will follow. We must prepare to join Victorio in his war to drive away the white soldiers who pretend to be warriors."

"The Mexicans who named you will not be pleased to know that El Gato is back."

The Mexicans had come to call him El Gato because of his preference for attacking in the darkness of the night, a nocturnal predator like the mountain cat. He had gladly adopted the name as his own and quickly discarded "Runs Fast," the name of his youth. El Gato was a warrior's name. "I will be staying behind until I capture the woman. You will lead the party to Mexico."

"You cannot do this. You are the leader of our band. And this woman. Have you considered what Cactus Bloom will say if you bring another wife to your lodge? If you must have another wife, her sister is entitled first."

"Her sister is ugly and as big and mean as a bear. The custom is not always followed. I would build another lodge for my second wife. Others do this. With our two daughters Cactus Bloom's lodge has become crowded. There would not be room for another wife. And I fear Cactus Bloom will not give me another son. I need another wife for this."

"Cactus Bloom will not be kind to a new wife."

"She will require time to become accustomed."

"At least ten summers, I would guess," Moon Watcher said.

El Gato's friend was starting to annoy him. "I have decided."

"I will stay with you. We have almost twenty warriors. One Hand can lead the others and take the captives to the mountain village. The band will wait there until Victorio departs the San Carlos reservation."

One Hand was an older warrior, several years past his fortieth birthday. He had lost his left hand to a soldier's sabre as a young man but bowed to none in his fierceness as a warrior and had developed wisdom and cunning to more than offset his physical impediment. El Gato had confidence that One Hand could carry out the mission.

"I will inform One Hand. Then I must sleep. You should also. We will take up the pursuit after the sun hides behind the mountains."

"Yes, I knew that would be El Gato's plan. Stalk the prey under the black shroud of the night."

Chapter 3

CAL RIVERS MADE a wide sweep of the forest behind the travelers and, satisfying himself that no pursuers were closing in, returned to the rear of the column. He trailed Tabby, who led the two mules and extra horse on a rope line, while North Star ranged nearly a hundred yards ahead on the well-established trail. Cal was confounded by the encounter with the Apaches. What were they doing this far north? They could not be up to any good. And this El Gato stalking Tabby troubled him. He chided himself for not picking up signs of the Apache earlier. The renegade must have been sneaking near the campsite in the evening or during the night.

He hoped that after losing two warriors El Gato and the remainder of any war party would turn back south. Surely the capture of one woman would not be worth the chase. Of course, he did have the furs he purchased from the strange and beautiful woman they encountered on the Apache Trail some days back. They would have some value but, again, not enough to justify following the owners into Navajo country. He had purchased the furs at a fraction of their market value, hoping he might garner a profit from this journey Tabby had invited him to share.

Tabitha reined in her gray gelding, Smokey, and the trailing animals slowed and stopped. Cal eased his big bay gelding past the train and sidled the horse up to Tabitha's mount. "What are you stopping for?" Cal asked his sister. She pointed up the trail toward North Star, who was riding his strawberry roan stallion their direction at a brisk trot. "North Star signaled a stop when I first caught sight of him coming this way."

"It must not be too serious. He's not pushing the roan."

When North Star approached his awaiting comrades, he slowed his stallion to a walk before stopping five paces in front of Cal and Tabitha. "Apaches were ahead of us," he said. "They struck a Navajo village about two miles down the trail four or five days back. I met up with a warrior who was watching the trail and explained that Tabby and I are mixed bloods looking for relatives among the Diné. His name is Delgado."

"Sounds Mexican," Cal said.

"After several centuries of war and occasional peace, many Navajo have names derived from the Spaniards and Mexicans, according to my mother," North Star said. His mother, Tabitha's Aunt Dezba, taught school near Taos and was a serious student of Navajo history. Tabitha was counting on her as an invaluable resource for her next book.

"Well," Tabitha said, "lead us to Delgado. It appears we're not arriving at a happy time."

North Star wheeled his mount, and started back down the trail, and the others fell in behind him. They had begun a steep descent from the mountains during the night. It was mid-morning now, and Cal had planned to call for a halt to rest riders and horses for a half day, but it sounded as if they were near a significant stop on their journey.

Soon they broke out of the woods onto a plateau that seemed to stretch to the horizon. Cal had noticed a thinning of trees and other vegetation as they exited the mountain slopes, but what lay ahead looked like near desert, broken up occasionally by a smattering of scrub oak and cottonwood, yucca and crisscrossing arroyos. At first glance the landscape seemed desolate, but a closer look revealed a fair scattering of livestock edibles, including sagebrush, buckbrush, bulrush and patches of squirreltail. He recognized mixed varieties of brome grass, and there were patches of other brown grasses he could not identify. He also knew from his scouting days in west Texas that an occasional oasis of green was likely to be found in the hidden canyons and valleys in such country.

Someone was watching from the pitiful-looking aspen grove behind them and off to their right. He supposed that the observer was Delgado verifying that the visitors looked harmless enough. Cal was not in a mood to pretend that he did not see the man and swung his bay around and waved. Shortly, a man astride a bay mare emerged from the trees. As he approached, the slim rider displayed a sheepish smile on his dark face. Except for the cloth band wrapped about his head, the man could have passed for one of the Santa Fe Mexicans with his cotton shirt and denim britches and ankle-high moccasins.

"I am Delgado," the man said. "Welcome to the land of the Diné. North Star says you come in peace."

Cal was taken aback with the man's English fluency, once again in awe of those who could shift from one language to another with such ease. He had grown up among Mexican vaqueros who worked on Levi Rivers's Slash R ranch but had picked up only a few common words and phrases. *Buenos dias. Adios. Si. Senorita.* Hell, by his siblings' standards, and to the consternation of his mother, he had barely mastered English. He nudged his horse forward to meet Delgado's and leaned over and extended his hand. "I'm Cal Rivers. Pleased to meet you."

The Navajo took his hand in a vice-like grip, and Cal had to consciously hold back flinching. "My pleasure, Cal," Delgado said.

Cal turned and saw that Tabby was riding up next to him. "Tab," he said, "this is Delgado."

Delgado nodded his greeting and rendered a small salute. "Welcome, ma'am. North Star tells me you are of the Diné."

"My mother was the daughter of Astsam, a full-blood Diné who came from this land. North Star is also the grandson of Astsam. His mother, Dezba, is Diné, and my late mother, Summer, whose Diné name was Doba, was Dezba's half-sister."

"Interesting names. Dezba in our tongue means 'war' and Doba is 'peace.'"

"Aunt Dezba thought she was given her name because of her birth during time of war and that my mother's name represented hope."

"That may well be, but until recent years, war with either the Mexicans, Americans or native tribes had been almost a constant state. We have enjoyed some years of peace since the Long Walk. Unfortunately, that has changed."

Cal said, "North Star says Apaches raided one of your villages."

"Yes. It is very sad." His face turned grim. "They killed and scalped two elders—a woman who was the matriarch of the Hawk clan and her husband. You should understand The People belong to the clan of their maternal line. The Apaches also murdered and mutilated her seventeen-year old grandson who resisted and tried to fight off the raiders. Three women were taken and two girls not more than a year from their moon times. My wife, Sunrise, was one of the women. My twelve-year old son, Fears Nothing, was captured also. The men and some of the older women were absent moving horses and goats to a blind canyon for grazing and building a fence to keep the animals enclosed. They were nearly three miles away and did not know of the attack until my ten-year old son, Stands Tall, who escaped, found them and reported what had happened. By the time they returned to the village, the Apaches had disappeared with their captives."

Tabitha said, "I am so sorry about your wife and son. Some of the village occupants escaped?"

"Yes. Still Water was helping a lambing ewe in an arroyo not far from the village. Five children were with her—they follow her like lambs trailing their mother. She heard the screams and gunfire and led the young ones down the arroyo to a hiding place and sent Stands Tall to summon the work party. Then she returned to the village to help the survivors until the others arrived. She said the raiders struck quickly and were gone by the time she reached the village. Given time, they probably would have killed everyone, but some hid in their hogans, and others scattered into the surrounding arroyos. They started to burn the hogans, but were somehow distracted and did not finish, so much of the village remains."

Cal said, "I think we ran into a few of the war party a few days back. They'll probably be heading to Mexico. Part of Victorio's Mimbres band. This bunch hightailed it off the reservation, I'd guess. That can't be a good sign of what's going on at San Carlos. I wonder if Victorio's on the loose again, too?"

"The Diné have warred with different Apache bands since ancient times, but not so much since we returned from the Bosque Redondo in 1868 during the time of the Long Walk. That has been eleven years now." Delgado said, "But follow me. I will take you to what remains of the village. Manuelito should be there now."

Delgado reined his horse past the visitors, and Cal and Tabitha fell in behind him. They joined North Star, who had remained with the spare horse and pack mules and then headed westward across the barren land. Cal edged his mount in close to Delgado's. "Who is Manuelito?" he asked.

"He is one of our chiefs; perhaps the most revered of those living. He was the last to surrender when the Diné were captured and herded like cattle on the long walk to Fort Sumner and the Bosque Redonda many miles from here. And Manuelito and Barboncito, who has joined his ancestors, were leaders in negotiating the 1868 Treaty that returned The People to their homeland. He was at the Canyon de Chelly and will bring warriors to pursue the raiders. I will join them."

"They have a good head start," Cal said, "but if the larger band was anywhere near those we ran into, they might not have gone as far as they could have." He told Delgado about the encounter with El Gato and the two warriors.

"That is very strange. You are fortunate you were not attacked by the main war party."

"We are. It don't make sense, but they're probably headed south now. I can lead you back to where we camped and probably pick up the war party's gathering place there. I had a fair amount of scouting experience during the Comanche wars, and I'd be glad to ride with you if this Manuelito is okay with it."

"He is not a prideful man. I am sure he would welcome your assistance. I and two others tried to pick up the trail but lost it when they went into the mountains. We also came to realize we could not release the captives if we found them. We were too few, and the Apaches were more likely to kill their prisoners if we could not strike and recover them quickly."

Soon Cal could make out the outlines of Navajo hogans on the horizon, and, shortly, human forms moving about the sprawling village came into view. As they approached, he now saw the charred remains of some of the structures and noted that the rebuilding process of some had already commenced. The structures seemed to be built in clusters, possibly arranged by family groups within the clan. The hogans appeared more varied and individual than the dwellings of other tribal villages he had seen. All had log frames and the dome-shaped roofs, most covered with sticks, bark and clay, but some of the walls simply continued the frame at a right angle to the ground, while others were vertical and made with clay-chinked logs in more the fashion of the white man's cabins. Some had a stone base that rose several feet above ground level.

As they reached the village, Cal caught sight of a gathering of a dozen or more men clad in variations of Delgado's garments just outside the east edge of the cluster of hogans. Several wore Mexican-style sombreros, and some wore Plainsman or low-crowned Stetson hats, but most preferred the bandana about the scalp attire. He was struck by the lack of conformity of dress among the Navajo.

"Manuelito is with the group of warriors. I see Still Water. I will introduce her, and Tabitha may stay with her while I take you and North Star to meet Manuelito. I will summon my son and his friends to tend to your horses."

Chapter 4

TABITHA WAS MIFFED by her exclusion from the warriors' gathering, but she conceded it was no different in her world until a woman busted through the male barrier and carved out her own place. In a few moments she shrugged off her irritation. Besides, Delgado had introduced her to an intriguing young woman who instantly made her feel she belonged to the damaged village and that regardless of her diluted blood, she was Diné.

Still Water could be no more than twenty years old, Tabitha guessed, but she carried herself with confidence and grace and was obviously wise beyond her years. She spoke flawless English, and Tabitha thought it strange that her first two Navajo encounters were with persons fluent in her own first language. Surely not all Diné were bilingual. She must find out about that.

Still Water stood a few inches shorter than Tabitha, making the young woman about five feet and three or four inches tall, Tabitha estimated. With soul-searching dark eyes and flawless bronze skin, she was a huge step beyond pretty and would turn the head of any but a blind male. Like Tabitha, Still Water wore buckskin britches this afternoon in contrast to most of the other women who wore skirts and blouses not unlike those most Mexican women wore in Santa Fe. There was so much to ask about these people. And to learn and eventually write. She had lived among the Comanche, the nomads of the plains, but this was a far different culture, it seemed.

Still Water said, "You will come to my hogan. I have no coffee, but we can have some tea and talk a bit. Then we can stroll about our village—or what remains of it."

Tea. The word triggered memories of Oliver, the Scotch-Cherokee artist she loved and had effectively deserted. He maintained a garden of herbs and harvested many in the wild to create gourmet blends of succulent teas. Coffee was kept in the home they shared only for guests who did not share their preferences. "I drink coffee only when there is no tea to be found."

"Wonderful. I think we are going to get on famously."

Odd, Tabitha thought. The remark sounded almost British.

When they arrived at the hogan, Tabitha noticed it was larger than most and was of log construction with the traditional dome roof. Like all the other structures, the doorway outlet was to the east, which she assumed had some religious or cultural significance. This home also had a skin-covered window opening on the south. As soon as they entered, Still Water went to the window and rolled up the skin and tied it in a roll with a leather strip attached for that purpose.

There were short benches on opposite sides of a fire pit encircled by stones. "Take a seat on one of the benches while I put the tea on," Still Water said.

Tabitha sat down and watched silently as Still Water stirred the coals in the pit with an iron rod to verify there was still heat. Then the Navajo woman retrieved a small metal pot and began filling it with liquid from a large pottery jug. Tabitha's eyes searched the room. There were two beds fashioned from wood poles, one on each side of the skin-covered entryway. They rose no more than two feet from the dirt floor and appeared to be covered with mattresses, probably grass-filled. Much of the room was taken up by shelves anchored to the walls and tables taking up floor space below. Bottles and pottery jars and bowls of various sizes occupied most of the shelves and tables, but Tabitha was surprised to see a sizable section of shelving set aside for a modest library. Her curiosity about this woman was becoming harder to contain.

"Tea's ready," Still Water said, handing Tabitha a steaming pottery mug before sitting down on the opposite bench.

"I'm sorry. Thank you. I was looking about your living quarters. This is . . . interesting."

Still Water laughed. "Different than your Comanche accommodations."

"Well, yes. But how did you know?"

"I know who you are." She set her mug on the bench and got up and went to her bookshelves, plucked two side-by-side books from a shelf and set them near the edge of the bench before picking up her mug and enjoying a sip of her tea before speaking again. "You are the Tabitha Rivers who wrote the unforgettable novel *The Last Hunt*." She held up one of the books that had that book's title emblazoned across the front cover. She put that book down and picked up the other. "And the nonfiction *Dismal Trail*. I am honored to have you as a guest in my modest home, Miss Rivers."

Tabitha flushed. "Please, call me Tabby. I hope you won't be offended, but the last thing I expected was to find my books on the Navajo reservation."

Still Water smiled. "I doubt if you will find many others within the 18,000 square miles of reservation lands. I read about your books in an old issue of the *Santa Fe Daily New Mexican* when I was teaching at the Navajo school near Fort Defiance two years ago. I went to great lengths to purchase them by mail, and I have read each book three or four times. They are simply fabulous. When I read *The Last Hunt,* I feel like I am living the last days of the Comanche with your protagonists. I hope you will have more books soon."

"That is partly why I came here—seeking a story waiting to be told."

"You must write about the Long Walk of the Diné. That's why I was so enraptured by your books. They reminded me of the trials endured by our people during that time."

"You would have been a child then."

Her face turned somber. "Oh yes, but I was there. This is 1879. The treaty that brought us home was signed in 1868. I was only nine years old and had been at the Bosque Redondo near Fort Sumner for almost five years. I was with the first of my people to arrive. My mother died during childbirth on the journey. My father was killed during an Apache raid two years later."

"You were orphaned?"

"You could say so, but the Hawk clan does not allow you to think that way. Others took me in, and life went on. I can speak dispassionately about it now but that has taken the passage of years to achieve. I was frightened and angry, but outwardly I remained calm and carried on, almost stoically, I guess it seemed to some. It was during the time at Fort Sumner that I became known as Still Water, alluding to my apparent calmness during those terrible times. I assure you my behavior did not reflect the inner turmoil."

"You obviously obtained a solid education somehow."

"Yes. A school was operated at Fort Sumner, and Navajo children were encouraged to attend. In fact, it was part of the government's plan to obliterate the Diné culture and turn our people into whites. Most resisted and refused to send their children. But I was curious and too little to be blinded by the politics of it all. My clan guardians said I could go or not. I was the youngest to show up for class. A few older children came at the insistence of parents who wisely thought the learning of the white man's words might be helpful someday. Delgado was one of those. He must have been twelve or thirteen and did not attend willingly, but as he learned, he quickly became a scholar who set the pace for all."

"What happened after the treaty signing and your return to the Diné lands? You would still have been a child."

"Fort Defiance established a boarding school, and several religious groups started schools there. Many Navajo families resisted, but Manuelito preached that the Diné children should be educated for times that lay ahead. He sent his own children away to the schools for six months out of the year, and several have attended other Indian boarding schools. I first went to Fort Defiance and then spent two years at the Josiah Missionary School maintained by Quakers at Fort Sill in the Indian Territory. When I returned, I taught for several years at Fort Defiance before coming home to my people to teach the children here, which had always been my plan."

"You teach, but the medicine bottles and containers on your shelves and tables suggest you also tend to medical needs."

"I do what I can. I have learned from Paloma, the ancient medicine woman of the clan, but I also have my books. My work is a blend of the time-tested knowledge of our people and the information imparted by trained physicians. The challenge is always to sort out what makes sense when the medical problem is presented. I have much to learn, but there is no alternative. Paloma has become feeble and cannot do much more than advise these days, and it would be a week's travel to seek aid at Fort Defiance, at least several days to locate a healer in another clan and bring him here."

"North Star and I wish to find relatives among the Diné. I would welcome your thoughts about where we might start. We are cousins but are both mixed bloods. North Star's mother, Dezba, is full blood Diné and was born in this land, as was my mother, her half-sister. Their mother's Navajo husband was killed when Dezba was a child and then she married my mother's father, who was a trader and took the family to Taos. My mother's Navajo name was Doba, but her father renamed her Summer. Aunt Dezba married a Pueblo, so North Star is half Pueblo. Summer died giving birth to me, and I was a love child. Do you understand what that means?"

Still Water smiled and nodded her head knowingly. "You have much company in this world."

"My father is an Anglo rancher of assorted European heritage—he calls himself a 'mongrel Texan.' So I would be only quarter-blood Navajo."

"You may consider yourself Diné if you choose. We are a people of mixed bloods. Spaniards, Mexicans, Anglos, Pueblo, Apache and many other tribes have contributed to our bloodlines. My mother's father was Spanish. To be Diné is something that comes from within you. The soul says you are Diné as much as the blood. But as to your relatives among the Diné, we should start with Paloma. If she does not have answers, she will tell you where to begin your search. I will take you to her tomorrow, but during your stay here, you will lodge in my hogan."

Chapter 5

TABITHA AND STILL Water emerged from the hogan just when the meeting with Manuelito was breaking up. Tabitha waved at Cal, and her brother, with North Star tagging behind, headed in her direction.

As they approached, Still Water said, "The Navajo man is the one you call North Star?"

"Yes, he is the one I told you about. I guess you did not see him when we rode in. I told you about his mother."

"Is he married?"

Tabitha turned to her new friend and caught the mischievous look in her eyes. "No, he is not married. He happens to be looking for a wife. Are you in the market for a husband?"

"No. No. I was courted by an Englishman at Fort Defiance—he was a captain in the American Army and quite charming. He taught me to dance. Of course, I would not leave the homeland, and that discouraged him. He still led me on, though, until one night he decided it was time for me to remove my pantaloons and tried to force himself upon me. He retreated with a face that looked like it had been mauled by a cougar. Now, I am on the verge of spinsterhood by Diné standards."

Tabitha laughed. But she noticed Still Water's eyes were still fixed on North Star and that her cousin was not oblivious to the young Navajo woman's presence.

When the two men reached the hogan, Tabitha introduced her companions. "Still Water, the giant is my brother, Cal Rivers, and the handsome stranger is my cousin, North Star. Gentlemen, meet Still Water, my new friend."

Cal nodded and said, "Pleased to meet you, Still Water."

North Star removed his hat and gave a slight bow. "My pleasure, ma'am."

Still Water replied. "I was looking forward to meeting you. Tabby has said so many nice things about you both."

Tabitha could not recall more than casually mentioning their names. "I won't be pitching my tent tonight. Still Water has offered me lodging in her hogan."

Still Water said, "There is a vacant hogan on the south side of the village where the two of you can store your gear and sleep. The young man who built it married into another clan and now lives in the village of his wife's family."

North Star said, "That would be good. If there is space, we can stack up Cal's furs there and stash our surplus supplies. We're riding out with Manuelito's outfit at sunrise to track the Apaches and try to get the captives back."

"The effort must be made," Still Water said, "but I fear that so much time has passed the task will be very difficult. But come with me, I will show you Chiqueto's empty lodge."

North Star stepped in front of Cal, brushing him aside and falling in beside Still Water. Cal looked at Tabitha and rolled his eyes and shrugged as brother and sister tagged along several paces behind. The leaders were engaged in quiet conversation and seemed oblivious to their companions.

Tabitha asked Cal, "Do you think you can catch the Apache war party?"

"Chances ain't good. If we do, it will be outside the Navajo homelands somewhere in the mountains to the south, probably across the Mexican border. We're too many to surprise anybody, and we'd be in the Apache band's lair. I don't like it. North Star interpreted for me—I didn't know he talked good Navajo—and I tried to convince Manuelito to let North Star and me and one of the Navajos find out where the war party went. Then we could plan a raid and not risk being bushwhacked. Manuelito wasn't buying any white man's suggestions. He seems like a good man. Just wary of strangers maybe. Probably has cause. Maybe if we get a scent, he'll change his mind if it's his idea."

"Just don't take off on your own. I don't want you to get yourself killed."

"Little Sis, since you and North Star got me sobered up, I figure I got some things to live for. I ain't going to risk my hide unless the odds are heavy in my favor."

That did not sound like the Cal she knew, but he would do what he pleased no matter what she said. Still Water and North Star stopped near one of the larger hogans. "This was Chiqueto's," she said. "He will trade it for some sheep or goats before winter, but until then, he said clan guests can use it. If you wish to leave him a few furs to show your appreciation, I am sure he would be grateful."

Cal said, "Sort of like room rent, I guess. Sure, I'd be glad to do that to have a place to store my things and not have to set up that ragged tent. I need to get rid of these furs. Where's the nearest trading post?"

"Fort Defiance. A three days' ride from here with a loaded pack mule. Two days without. I need supplies at Defiance, and a small caravan from here will be going to the fort within the week. I can market the furs for you if you like."

"I smell a business deal. What do you get out of it?"

"Ten percent."

"You a good trader?"

"Yes. And I will accept only gold coinage in payment."

"Okay. Do it."

"After you are settled, come to my hogan for supper. I will have lamb stew with roasted corn and frybread."

"That sounds delicious," North Star said enthusiastically.

Cal was stone-faced, but Tabitha knew he would welcome an excuse to escape. He was a big, tough man, but he had always been a fussy eater, confining his meat menu to beef, bison or venison. Pork in the form of ham or bacon was also on his approved list.

Later, as the sun slipped below the horizon, and night started to drop its blanket over the plateau, Tabitha sat alone in the hogan, planted on the bench next to the fire pit that radiated welcome warmth from the red-hot embers that covered the bottom. The day's warmth on the desert-like flatlands, like in the mountains, gave way to an unpleasant chill even as June closed in on July.

She smiled to herself as she thought of Cal valiantly dipping his frybread into the lamb stew and swallowing it quickly before washing it down with a drink from his canteen. He had seemed to find it more palatable after the first few bites. She had thought the meal delicious, but she had lived with the Comanche during a bleak winter when they were being starved out by the Army. Cut off from buffalo, deer, and other traditional food sources, they had turned to dogs, horses, and any wild thing that moved for a food supply.

North Star had enjoyed the meal and had rarely taken his eyes off Still Water. He was obviously enamored of her, and she had seemed more than casually interested in her cousin. At his invitation, she was strolling with him now. It made her lonely for Oliver Wolf and saddened again by the cowardly way she had fled from his life—their life. She wondered how long it would be before he found another to love. She envisioned a line of young women outside Oliver's beautiful home waiting for the opportunity to seduce the Adonis who was becoming an artist of increasing renown. She found herself jealous of these faceless women.

What was Oliver doing tonight? She knew what they would likely be doing if she were with him. She tried, but she could not erase the image of his naked body moving in total harmony with her own, giving and the taking of mutual pleasure, all a bonus to the mind that challenged her and the words that calmed. She loved him, and he had loved her. Tonight, she was close to abandoning the quest, the purpose of which was growing increasingly jumbled in her mind.

The buckskin doorway flap rustled, and Tabitha was yanked from her reverie. Still Water slipped through the opening and took a place on the opposite bench. Tabitha waited for her new friend to say something.

After a few moments of silence, Still Water's lips surrendered traces of a sheepish grin. "I apologize for being a poor hostess. It seems North Star and I could not stop talking."

"Don't apologize. I'm glad you found something in common."

"I don't know that we have so much in common. It was the differences I found intriguing. He was raised among the Pueblo, but his mother gave him the soul of Diné. I was shocked to find him so fluent in the Diné language. And he is very well read and knowledgeable on many subjects."

"I am sorry to say that I hardly know him. I did not know of my own Navajo heritage until little more than a year ago. Until he joined us on our journey, I had only met him briefly on a few occasions when I visited Aunt Dezba. But I have come to respect him. I don't know what I would have done if he had not appeared when Cal was having a crisis with demon alcohol. I am proud to be his cousin."

"He has a small horse ranch near Taos, and he breaks and trains horses for others. But he seems very sophisticated in the ways of commerce. And he is very ambitious."

"You are beginning to sound like a woman smitten."

She shrugged and smiled. "You won't tell him?"

"Of course not."

"There was something about him when I first set my eyes on him. He is quite handsome, but it was the way he carried himself. Confident, quiet and calm."

Tabitha laughed. "And you say you have little in common?"

"I just hope I have an opportunity to know him better. I know it is necessary, but I hate to see him ride out on the search in the morning."

"I gather you have no male interest at the moment?"

"No. None since the Englishman at Fort Defiance I told you about. Young men my age seem shy about approaching me, and the desirable older ones have been claimed. I am not concerned about finding a husband now, perhaps ever. It is customary that we marry outside our clan and that the husband become a part of the wife's clan. This makes it more difficult to find a match, especially if one does not participate in the interclan social gatherings. I usually prefer the company of my books. Some men—not all—take two or more wives. No thank you. Now, it is not unheard of for a wife to take an additional husband, but men seem to have more trouble accepting that practice. I do think one would be sufficient."

"Yes, I agree. I left behind a man who asked me to marry him."

"You loved him?"

"Yes. I still do. Any other man I ever meet will be judged against Oliver's qualities and found lacking."

"So why did you not marry him?"

"That is the question I was asking myself before you returned. Why did I not marry him?"

Chapter 6

EL GATO AND Moon Watcher lay in a cluster of sagebrush and boulders not more than a hundred yards from the Hawk clan's principal village site. They watched with interest as the search party rode away from the village.

"They think they are going to reclaim our captives," El Gato said. "One Hand is days ahead of them by now, and he is a wily old warrior. He will disappear into the Mexican mountains before they find any sign."

Moon Watcher said, "I know the Navajo who leads them. I saw him once at Fort Defiance. He is a chief or high-ranking warrior. Manuelito. He was the last resister during the time the whites herded the Navajo to the Bosque Redondo on what they call the Long Walk. He is known as a fierce warrior and is said to be very cunning. He should not be underestimated."

"He is not our concern. Not now. We must think on taking the woman."

"We should think on joining One Hand and our band in Mexico."

"Five Suns. If we cannot take her in five suns, we will go."

"There are armed men left in the village, we cannot enter safely and capture her there. She appears to share a lodge with another woman. We might kill that one, but to steal into the village and the lodge and attempt to do so quietly carries great risk."

Once more, El Gato found himself wishing that Moon Watcher had not accompanied him. Still, accomplishing the woman's capture without his help would be more difficult, perhaps impossible. "We will continue to watch. Our opportunity will come."

Chapter 7

AS TABITHA AND Still Water watched the search party disappear in a hovering cloud of dust, Still Water said, "Tomorrow, we will join others on a journey to Fort Defiance for supplies. I will take the furs and sell them at the trading post near there."

"How long will this take?"

"A day and a half travel each way without pushing the horses and allowing for ample rest and one overnight stay near Dripping Springs. We should make the fort by early the second afternoon."

"Dripping Springs?"

"A small canyon that is approximately midway between here and the fort. Water seeps out one of the sandstone walls and drips into a pool that overflows and feeds a stream that runs almost the length of the canyon before it disappears underground. There is grass on the canyon floor and ample water for riders and animals."

"How many will go with us?"

"Probably two other women and their husbands and two sons not far from manhood—old enough to engage in battle in the unlikely event we should encounter trouble."

"And I will have my Henry rifle."

"And I, my Winchester."

"Is it usual for Navajo women to use firearms?"

"It is not uncommon. Most can use them even if they do not carry their own weapons. Since the Long Walk, all are prepared for war. We will never leave this land again. It is better to die in this place defending it."

"I must learn about the Long Walk."

"I will take you to Paloma this afternoon. She can give you the perspective of an ancient. She has seen ninety springs, so she was not a youngster. I will tell you what I remember, but you will want to talk to many. I will be disappointed if you do not surpass your novel *The Last Hunt* with your narrative. It will be a novel, will it not?"

"Yes. But there may be a non-fiction work here also."

"Like your works about the last days of the Comanche?"

"Yes, perhaps."

"That would be wonderful."

"I have much to learn before I start to write."

Later, Tabitha and Still Water sat on the rough ground under an arbor fashioned from tree branches and dry grass in front of Paloma's hogan. The wizened woman sat on a stool lashed together from small sticks and rawhide strips. Paloma had doubtless been a tiny woman in her youth, Tabitha thought, but she doubted if she would weigh ninety pounds. Her body was failing but her mind and memory remained keen. Paloma spoke little English, so Still Water interpreted while the three conversed. Tabitha took notes as they spoke, and the elderly woman seemed fascinated as Tabitha put pencil to paper.

"Did all the Diné make the Long Walk?" Tabitha asked. She waited as Still Water translated, and Paloma gave a response that lasted for some minutes.

When Paloma finished, she nodded and gave Tabitha a toothless smile. Still Water spoke, "Paloma says there were some who remained hidden in the canyons and did not go, but not many. The Long Walk was a collective name given to many so-called walks, probably more than fifty over the three years from 1863 to 1866. And they were not 'walks' in any real sense. They were forced marches of clans captured by the white soldiers and herded like sheep from our land to the Bosque Redondo and Fort

Sumner. Those who were not strong enough to make the journey were left to die along the trail. Many old people just walked away from the procession and disappeared in the desert. Women giving birth and those who were ill or injured were left behind to catch up or not. She gave me examples and names, which I can provide later if you wish."

"That would be good. I don't want to tax her strength. And, perhaps we can talk again when we return from Fort Defiance. Ask her to tell me about the destination, the Bosque Redondo."

Again, Still Water posed the question, and the old woman rambled on. Suddenly, she stopped speaking and tears rolled down her cheeks. She turned her face away.

Still Water said, "The place was flat and barren. Trees were rare, even along the river's bank. The water source was the river's alkaline water, and the army distributed spoiled and rancid meat for rations. They had not been permitted to bring their own sheep and cattle on the journey, and only a few horses. The land grew nothing edible. They could not see the mountains from this place, and it made them sicker for home. They were left without weapons to defend against raids by Comanche and Apache war parties. Her two sons died trying to defend the clan during such attacks. Her granddaughter was abducted by Comanche. Another granddaughter died during childbirth, and her surviving child died from a white man's disease. When the Treaty of 1868 was signed, she was the only survivor of her family. The bones of her loved ones remain in that white man's hell."

They talked for several hours, and then Tabitha saw that Paloma was tiring. "Tell her that we must go now and that I hope she will allow me to visit again after we return from Fort Defiance."

Tabitha stood while Still Water explained and stepped toward the ancient woman and placed a hand on her shoulder. "Thank you," she said. "The story of the Long Walk must be told and printed on the white man's paper, so such a thing will not happen again."

Still Water translated, and Paloma looked up at Tabitha with teary eyes, nodding her head in approval.

Upon returning to Still Water's hogan, the Navajo woman said, "I can write much of this down, if it would help. I can talk to others and record what they say. I think the journalists call it interviews."

"That would be wonderful. I have so much to learn and would gladly compensate you for it."

"Oh, money would not be necessary. This is something I would do for my people, and I will tell my own family's story."

"We can discuss money another time. This has become more than I can comprehend. I need help with this project. You can be my researcher."

Chapter 8

THE TRIP TO Fort Defiance had been uneventful. As anticipated, the Hawk clan's trading party arrived at the fort early afternoon of the second day. The next morning, Tabitha accompanied Still Water on a visit to the fort's trading post where the young Navajo entrepreneur marketed the furs at a price that left the trader grumbling.

Outside the trading post, Still Water introduced Tabitha to a young Navajo man a few years older than her Santa Fe friend. He had attended school with her as a child at Fort Sumner during the years of the Long Walk and again at the Fort Defiance school. Chee Dodge worked as a contract interpreter at the fort, and the Diné called him "Man Who Understands Languages." Dodge was fluent in English and Spanish besides his native Navajo and spoke passable Apache and Hopi. Still Water said the young man did not hesitate to capitalize on his language skills and had a nose for financial opportunities. His mother was of the Coyote Pass clan, but the identity of his father was uncertain, likely Mexican or Spanish, according to Still Water.

Tabitha found Chee Dodge charming and noted that Still Water and the young interpreter had a relaxed and flirtatious relationship. He was a lanky man of above average height and wore a fringed buckskin coat that Tabitha found a bit flamboyant for the rustic frontier environment. He was somewhat loquacious for her taste, but she liked him and thought there might be a handsome face beneath the long scraggly moustache that he was trying to maintain with foliage that was too sparse. Upon learning of Tabitha's plans to write about the Long Walk, Chee seemed delighted to tell her more than she needed to know about what he remembered of his experiences as a child during that time.

Chee said, "I know a few soldiers stationed here that could tell you how the other side saw things. If you get back this way and can stay a few days, I'll be glad to introduce you."

"That would be wonderful. I'll plan to take you up on your offer."

"If you should mention me in your book, my full name is Henry Chee Dodge."

"You will no doubt be mentioned, so I will write that down."

The two women moved on, strolling toward the fort proper, Still Water leading the mule which had been relieved of its burden. Still Water said, "Your brother said he would give me a commission on the mule, too, if I could sell it. We'll go to the Army's stables. They're usually short of four-legged critters, and they will give her good care. Defiance rarely has troops in the field these days, so she won't get overworked or eaten by Apaches."

Tabitha said, "Your friend Chee was an interesting man. No potential romance?"

Still Water giggled. "No. We're just longtime friends. We had a brief infatuation in our early teenage years, but he was too outgoing, and I was too quiet and reserved. We made each other crazy. There was never any spark between us in the romantic way. I enjoy male friends who know the friendship is not going beyond that. Do you understand?"

"Oh, yes. It gets very complicated when that friendship has already gone beyond."

"Like with your friend, Oliver?"

Tabitha sighed. "Yes, like my friend, Oliver." And lover. And sanctuary.

"After I sell the mule, we could head back to the village if you wish. I only have a few purchases to make. Without the pack mule slowing us we could make Dripping Springs by nightfall."

"What about the others?"

"They will likely stay over until tomorrow. We could relax a day at Dripping Springs and wait for them to catch up."

Tabitha found the suggestion inviting. The overnight stay at the springs had left her wishing she had time to explore the area. The canyon was an oasis in a desert carpeted with lush grass and ample shade offered by scattered cottonwoods along the stream that knifed through the valley between the canyon walls. "Yes," she said, "let's do that. I would love the chance to see more of the canyon."

A half hour later, Still Water negotiated sale of the mule to the Army. She also purchased a black white-stockinged mare from a miner that she thought she could sell for a nice profit to a horse trader in the Hawk clan. They stopped by the commandant's office to complete a bill of sale and payment voucher for the mule and a stack of papers that seemed to have little relevance to the transaction. When the paperwork was finalized, Still Water complained some about the eighty dollars in paper money tendered in payment. As they walked out the door, she commented, "Maybe Cal will take the paper with his share. I prefer the gold double eagles we got for the furs."

"He brought a saddle bag of gold coinage with him. He doesn't need more weight to carry. I think he would be agreeable. When he gets back to Santa Fe, there will be a fair number of businesses that don't mind taking paper."

The women rode away from Fort Defiance well before noon and moved across the flatlands of the plateau quickly until late afternoon when Tabitha's gray gelding, Smokey, came up lame. They reined in and dismounted, and Tabitha examined the gelding's left front foot that the horse seemed to be favoring. She discovered a wound in the flesh of the ankle just above the hoof. The cut leaked blood and appeared fresh, likely a gash from one of the sharp stone shards that littered the terrain. There was a bit of swelling, and Tabitha figured it would get worse before it got better, but with good care the damage would not be crippling, and the horse would recover.

"I'll clean up the wound when we get to Dripping Springs." Tabitha said. "A day's rest will help a lot. Do you suppose I could ride your new mare?"

"Of course."

They unsaddled Smokey and hitched the gelding to the lead rope and then saddled the new mare. The horse seemed in good shape for a miner's animal. She certainly had not been a load-bearing animal. Tabitha concluded her friend had made a good purchase.

"Doesn't it seem strange to you that a miner would own a fine horse like this? The mare obviously hasn't been used as a beast of burden," Tabitha said.

"He said the horse wandered into his camp a few weeks back. I will be charitable and take him at his word."

"Smokey's still going to slow us down. We won't make Dripping Springs until long after sunset."

"There is no other place to set up camp where there is shelter and water. At least it will be cooler riding as the sun sets."

As the sun dropped behind the horizon and gray dusk gave way to the blackness of night, Tabitha slowed her mount. "Wait," she said. "Did you hear that?"

Still Water reined in her gelding. "Hear what?"

"A horse's whinny."

"I didn't hear it. But it would not be unusual. There are wild horse herds roaming Diné land. And sound carries a great distance here. Or there could be other travelers passing this way."

"That's what spooks me. The other travelers."

"There is no one among The People who would bring us harm, I assure you."

"That's not my concern. I was thinking of Apaches." A chill raced down her spine, and her body tensed. "I told you about the warrior El Gato who was going to take me."

"It seems likely he would be far from here by now—with the war party that struck our village and took the women and children."

"Possibly," Tabitha said, doubtfully.

"We are not more than an hour from Dripping Springs. There are hiding places and caves in the canyon that we can defend until others arrive tomorrow. We must pick up the pace."

"If he has been following us, he knows where we are headed."

"The horses need rest. They are not going to outrace anyone. Dripping Springs is our only choice. Besides, our imaginations are probably creating our worries."

"Probably, but let's ride."

Chapter 9

A NEAR HALF-MOON AND a sprinkling of stars cast some light on the canyon floor, but eerie shadows danced everywhere, and half of them looked like lurking Apaches to Tabitha. They rode their horses at a walk into the canyon's mouth. Tabitha tossed a nervous glance over her shoulder to confirm that there was no rider closing in on them from behind. She nudged her horse up next to Still Water's.

"Let's go deeper into the canyon and find high ground, so we can keep an eye out."

"I know a cave in the wall about fifteen feet above the canyon floor. We could stake out the horses further upstream from here and circle back. It's an easy climb to the cave."

They dismounted and led the horses northerly into the canyon, hurrying along the bank edging the narrow ribbon of gurgling water. Still Water paused and pointed to a cluster of boulders along the west canyon wall. "There. Above the rocks we will find the cave and hide there."

Tabitha guessed the distance was no more than one hundred fifty feet. Increasingly, she was convinced they were not fleeing from illusory phantoms. "I say we go for the cave now and unsaddle the horses and turn them loose. They won't stray far—I know Smokey won't—and we can round them up in the morning."

"All right."

They unsaddled the horses and stashed what they did not need under an ancient gnarled cottonwood tree. They snatched up their rifles and saddlebags and were ready to race for the cave when the cracks of two rifle shots echoed off the canyon walls. Still Water spun around and collapsed. Tabitha's eyes searched the canyon, but she could not even make a guess as to where the shots came from. She knelt beside her friend and gave a sigh of relief when she saw Still Water was alive.

"Where are you hit?" she asked.

"Shoulder. Hip. I think. Run. Find cover."

"I can't just leave you here."

"You can't help me if they take you down. Run. If he chases you, I will try to crawl away. If you can find a hiding place, maybe you can kill him. You must kill. Apaches fight till death."

The horses had taken off with the gunfire. Tabitha decided to stay with the stream and continued the course they had been following, grateful that she was racing on moccasin-ed feet instead of the cowboy boots she sometimes wore. She could hear someone crashing through the trees and brush behind her. She reached a cluster of small cottonwoods and swung around, raising her Henry to fire. She saw the half-naked warrior coming on, but he dropped flat to the ground just as she fired. She lowered her aim, but before she could squeeze the trigger, she felt the presence behind her, and a powerful arm clamped about her neck, squeezing like a vice until she dropped her weapon and blacked out.

When Tabitha regained consciousness, she lifted herself to her knees and tried to remember what had happened. Her vision was hazy, and her neck and shoulders felt like they were being stabbed with needles, but she recognized one of the two warriors gazing down at her with impassive faces. El Gato. In the darkness, she could not make out the fine details of their features, but El Gato's eyes were unforgettable, paler than those of most Indians with a yellowish cast that almost seemed to glow in the moonlight. Like a cougar's eyes.

As she got to her feet, El Gato spoke. "Ta-Bee come. No hurt. Run, fight. El Gato hurt, kill."

She nodded and replied with a nod of her head.

As they moved away from the stream, she saw that the Apaches had captured her black, white-stocking mare and retrieved the saddle and bridle that had been used for Still Water's gelding. She worried about Smokey. Would the gelding survive on his own in this rugged, unforgiving land? And Still Water. What had they done with her? "My friend. Where is she? You bastards shot her." She was regaining her senses now, and rage was starting to consume her.

El Gato gestured toward the mare, "Ride horse. Go."

The Apache's English vocabulary seemed scant, but a single word was more than the Apache she spoke. What choice did she have? She stumbled over to the waiting mare hitched to one of the spindly trees in the nearby grove. She was surprised to see her prized Henry rifle in its saddle scabbard. She considered breaking loose and making a race for freedom after she mounted. All she needed was a small lead, and she could turn and take them down with the rifle. They would have no idea how proficient she was with the weapon.

As if reading her mind, El Gato said, "No bullets. My gun." He pointed at her. "My woman."

Like hell. She would never be his woman. And she would be damned if the devious son-of-a-bitch was going to steal her Henry. She mounted the mare that in her mind she now called "Socks." El Gato, with the grace of his namesake, leaped onto his calico stallion and eased onto the pad that formed the Apache's barebones saddle. He signaled that she should follow, and the other warrior, astride a chestnut gelding, fell in behind her.

The riders bypassed the place where the women had been ambushed and Still Water wounded. She did not see Still Water's body, but it could be hidden in the darkness. Tabitha took some consolation in the fact she saw no sign of a bloody scalp hanging from either Apache's belt. It gave her hope that Still Water might still live. But any assistance would be another day away, and she knew that her friend's survival was doubtful. They had been such fools to head back to the village without the others.

Chapter 10

STILL WATER SAT with her back resting against the cave's cold, rough sandstone wall. Her hiding place barely qualified as a cave, as her body took up nearly half of the grotto's capacity, but a rock overhang jutting from the steep canyon wall above the opening offered extra shelter and cover from searching eyes. The rising sun cast some light and a bit of welcome warmth over the canyon floor now. But, more importantly, the erasure of the night chased away some of her fear. She could finally begin to see and figure out what danger awaited her in the canyon.

She had half-crawled and half-run to the cave after Tabby left her. She wondered now if they should have stayed together. She thought Tabby had probably ended up serving as a decoy to enable her own escape. She had heard a shot fired as she was struggling to climb the short but steep trail to her refuge. But somehow, she did not think Tabby had been killed. It made no sense that the Apache would have stalked her this long only to take her life. He had some other purpose. Whether serving that purpose might be better than death, Still Water could not guess.

She decided she should leave the cave so the others of her clan would find her when they arrived. Corn Grower, a seasoned warrior, would be with them, and he could lead a search to determine if Tabby was lying dead in the canyon somewhere. Still Water did not think she would die of her wounds. The left shoulder throbbed with pain that raced down her arm, but the bullet had passed through the flesh between her neck and shoulder, and the bleeding had been staunched by strips of cloth torn from her shirt. If the Apache had not taken her saddlebags, she had powders there that would ease the pain and help ward off putrefaction, a threat from even the most insignificant wound. The lead was still lodged in her left hip, but she was confident that it had not struck bone and was lodged in the meat that merged into her buttocks. She still had her knife in its belt sheath, but she needed better light to examine the wound. With one gimpy arm it would be a challenge to remove the bullet herself. She could wait for assistance. It was better, however, to extract it sooner than later.

The cave ceiling was no more than four and one-half feet high and the opening smaller, so, after clutching her Winchester, she moved to her hands and knees to crawl out. The sun blinded her for a few moments, and she waited for her eyes to adjust before she slid down the path on her uninjured hip. Reaching the canyon floor, she was relieved to find that she could stand and walk slowly without incurring pain exceeding her ability to endure it. Hobbling at a turtle's pace, she reached the cottonwood tree where they had left their tack and gear. It appeared that the only thing missing was the saddle and riding gear for her own horse, but Tabby's saddle and bridle had been left untouched, and she could have someone put it on any horse that remained if the Apaches had not taken them all.

She snatched up her saddlebags and canteen, pressed her back against the tree trunk, and slid to the ground. She leaned back and took a few moments to rest and collect her thoughts. The day was young, and her clansmen would not arrive much before nightfall. Each hour the wounds were left unattended increased her risk of putrefaction and death. It was too dangerous to wait. She opened her saddlebags and, after confirming the gold coins from fur sales had not disappeared, rummaged through her little bags of powders, plucking out the one she was seeking.

She washed her shoulder wound with water from her canteen, using the contents sparingly since she would require more of it later. She was sitting only a few steps from the stream but preferred to avoid that water, thinking that the springs that streamed from the sandstone canyon wall at the water's source would be uncontaminated and that she could replenish her supply later.

After cleaning both the entry and exit sides of the shoulder wound, Still Water sprinkled powder from the doeskin bag on both sides of the wound and covered the blood-seeping holes with more strips of cloth again harvested from her shirt, the sticky discharge creating an adhesive. Her saddle blanket would furnish cover till help arrived.

She tugged her buckskin britches down over her hips, so she could evaluate the damage rendered by the second bullet. The pulsating in her hip reminded her that the injury was there, but the pain did not approach that of the shoulder wound. She studied the wound, fully displayed now by the beams from the morning sun. She stretched her right arm across her abdomen to confirm her fingers could reach the wound and maneuver her knife blade.

She found she had adequate movement in her left arm and hand to help manipulate the flesh.

She removed the knife from its sheath, washed the blade and rubbed her herbal powder over the gleaming steel, before wiping it clean. The blade of the bone-handled knife was narrow and razor-sharp, not used by Still Water as a skinning tool or weapon, but as a surgical instrument of sorts for lancing boils or other minor surgeries required by her people—only rarely for arrow or bullet wounds. More often, it was a tool for cutting or punching holes in leather.

As she inched the blade toward the puckered entry wound, she noted that bleeding was almost non-existent, which she found odd. The fingers of her left hand explored the wound and the flesh surrounding it, and she was certain she could feel the lead slug buried shallowly beneath the skin. She spread the wound open with her fingers and inserted the blade's point. After recovering from the initial shock of pain and resulting nausea that ripped through her as blade bit flesh, she began to probe, pushing the agony aside, while she located the slug and lifted with the blade point, using her fingers to manipulate it to the surface until it suddenly popped free and she passed out.

Some ten minutes later, she awakened to find her hip, thigh and britches blood-soaked but the ugly wound now only dripping the scarlet fluid. She considered the bleeding a positive occurrence. She had nothing with which to stitch the wounds, and her lame shoulder, hampered further by necessity of cross-body reach, would not have permitted such delicate work. She could wait till the others came to assist with that.

After she powdered and crudely dressed the hip wound, Still Water fell asleep again for several hours, awakening with a start when she heard the whinnying of a horse. Instinctively, she reached for her rifle, sighing with relief when she saw Tabby's gelding, Smokey, watching from no more than twenty feet distant. Her own horse was grazing not far away. Bracing against the tree, she stood up, taking time to recover from a wave of dizziness before she coaxed the horses her way. Smokey did not hesitate, and, shortly, her gelding followed its new friend's example.

Still Water felt stronger now, and the appearance of the horses started to alter her thinking. She would lose a full day if she waited for the arrival of the rest of the trade party, and it was even possible the others would extend their stay at the fort an extra day. Not knowing of the attack on herself and Tabby, they had no reason to rush.

She had to get word to the Diné pursuit party of Tabby's capture as soon as possible. Every hour was critical, and she could not help her friend waiting here. It would be a struggle to get her horse saddled and mounted in her condition, but she would do it. With luck she could reach the village before sunset.

IT WAS AFTER midnight when Still Water reached the village, only vaguely hearing barking dogs followed by the excited voices of people rushing from the hogans. She tumbled off her horse into the arms of a young warrior, and she was foggily aware of being carried. She heard Paloma's sing-song voice and felt soft hands feathering over the flesh about her wounds. The glow of the oil lantern she only occasionally used blinded her momentarily when she opened her eyes a few hours later. She was lying on the bed in her hogan, Paloma's somber wrinkled face hovered above her, the old woman's hand pressing a cool wet cloth against Still Water's forehead.

Paloma, speaking Navajo, said, "You are safe quiet one, and I have stitched your wounds, leaving an opening for the poisons to escape. I will care for you, and time will bring your strength back."

"Tabby has been taken by Apaches. I must speak to the senior warrior."

"I saw our relative's gray horse following yours. I feared something terrible had happened. I will summon Nez. You may tell him."

The ancient woman shuffled out the entryway. Still Water noticed that the pain from her gunshot wounds had subsided noticeably. She credited that to potions Paloma had no doubt administered. She made no effort to test her mobility. She felt relaxed, like she might be drifting on a cloud, and she preferred to savor the sensation. Her body was coaxing her to sleep, but she fought off the tug to peaceful oblivion. She must speak with Nez first.

Soon Paloma returned with Nez, a warrior Still Water knew to be in his late thirties and a good horseman whose advice and assistance were sought when a horse, goat, cow or other animal was injured or ailing. He had lost his first wife and son during the Long Walk and later married his wife's younger sister with whom he started a new family. He was a handsome man notwithstanding a missing ear that had been amputated by a white Army officer's sabre during the walk to the Bosque Redondo.

"Still Water," he said, kneeling beside her bed and speaking Navajo, "I am sorry for your injuries, but I am happy to confirm that you are alive. Paloma says you will recover, and that pleases me, as well as all members of the clan. She insisted that I come speak with you. What is it? How can I help?"

"I assume you have heard the story and know that our relative from the east was taken by Apaches? Two of them, I think."

"Yes, I have heard."

"We must get word to our war party. Tabby's brother and cousin must know of this. And she should be included in any search. Can you send a messenger to find them?"

"I will be the messenger. I fought for Manuelito during the resistance. I know his ways, and he will listen to me."

"Thank you, my friend. I knew I could depend upon you." Her last words were slurred as she closed her eyes and dropped off to sleep.

Chapter 11

TABITHA CLUNG TO the saddle horn with one hand and clutched the reins in the other, giving her mare the lead to follow El Gato's stallion. She still suffered spells of dizziness from the choking-arm clamp El Gato had applied to her neck and throat, and the lack of sleep was taking its toll. The first rays of sunlight were slipping over a spiny ridge in the east. They traveled mostly at night, which seemed to be more the Apache's preference than a strategy. The daytime heat was not unbearable, and her captors had no difficulty locating water sources, although most would have been invisible to a greenhorn's eye.

They were completing the second night of her abduction, and she had slept little and eaten less. She felt like screaming at the bastards. She wanted to cry but would not give them the satisfaction. The only conversation had been between the two Apaches in their language, which was gibberish to her. She knew El Gato spoke rudimentary English but not enough for serious dialogue. Regardless, her questions obviously annoyed him and were greeted with stony silence. She gave up and focused on how she might survive this ordeal.

Tabitha had no idea why her capture had been so important to El Gato that he had followed her to the Navajo village and beyond. She took some solace in the fact they had not harmed her beyond a few shoves on the back or rough yanks on her arms to direct her to sit down or gather firewood or perform some other chore. She had no doubt it would take very little to trigger violence on El Gato's part. He was clearly the leader, but from the tone of his voice it seemed the other Apache was unafraid to give his opinion when he deemed it necessary. El Gato's companion, however, seemed calmer and more deliberate in his ways.

Mid-morning, they approached a cluster of scrub pines and a stone outcropping with a spiny ridge that arched abruptly from the barren land and extended some thirty feet before burrowing back into the earth. El Gato led the riders to the east side of the ridge signaling to her they would probably sleep here and claim the stone wall's shade from the scorching afternoon sun.

When they dismounted, she observed tufts of tall green grass sprouting amidst a jumble of large stones near a crevice in the wall. Tabitha knew this signaled a water source vital to man and beast.

El Gato dismounted and for the first time in a day spoke English to her. "Down. Blanket. Tree." He pointed to the spindly pines that were rooted into the sand and rocks no more than thirty feet south from a small pool of water that she now saw had formed just outside the crack in the rock wall.

Tabitha did not object to spreading her blanket at his directed location. There was a bit of shade offered by the trees, and a shadow would be cast from the outcropping come afternoon. She just wanted to drop off into a long slumber. She was so exhausted she could not think clearly. And hungry. The little she had eaten had not come near to satisfying her hunger. The chunk of unknown mixture of meat and other substances had been similar in appearance to the Comanche's pemmican, for which she had acquired a fondness during her stay with Quanah's band. But the texture of this offering had been gristly and grainy, and the taste bitter. She had decided she would prefer not to know the contents.

After laying out the blanket, she returned to her mare and unsaddled the mount before leading her to the pool to drink. She had quickly been made to understand that the horse's care was her responsibility. Casting a sideways glance as she waited for the horse to drink its fill, she saw that El Gato's eyes were fixed upon her, as he and the other warrior staked out their horses in the grass not more than twenty-five feet distant to the north of the pool. She turned her head away until Socks had drunk her fill and then led the horse to the stand of grass and staked her near the others. That finished, she cast her eyes about the area, wondering if her captors would object if she returned to the trees and collapsed upon her blanket.

She saw that another blanket lay at the base of the escarpment not far from where the horses were staked. Nearby, El Gato appeared to be arguing with his cohort about something, the other man finally shrugged and turned away and dropped to the blanket, evidently planning to nap. El Gato started walking deliberately in Tabitha's direction. As he approached, those strange, gold-tinted eyes caused her to shudder. They were narrowed and purposeful, and she sensed that the purpose did not bode well for her.

When he reached her, he clutched her wrist before she could step back. "Ta-Bee my woman."

"What do you mean?" She tried to pull away, but his steel grip did not give an inch. She knew instantly what he meant.

El Gato did not reply. He started dragging her toward the trees where she had laid out her blanket. When they reached the spot, he released her. He grabbed the waist of her britches, yanking them down one hip, and then stepped back, signing that she was to remove her clothing. He demonstrated by tugging off the deerskin war shirt he wore during the chill of their night rides.

"No," she said and, while he was removing his shirt, started running for the horses. She would ride Socks bareback and run off the other mounts, they would never catch her. It did not matter that she had no idea where she was or where she might flee. She just wanted to escape from this place and this man.

Like his namesake, El Gato took her down quickly and rolled her over and straddled her, his fist driving into the side of her face like a warclub. Dazed from the blow, her arms flailed as the Apache began tearing off her shirt. When her head cleared, she saw he was standing and had just finished pulling off her britches. She felt the sand and dirt grating her back. Now he knelt and started ripping away her cotton underpants. His breechclout and skinning knife lay on the ground within her reach. She closed her eyes momentarily when she saw the turgid manhood swinging from his loins. She rolled away, and her arm stretched for the knife, her fingers closing on the hilt. She swung the blade around to strike and carved a shallow groove in his shoulder before he grabbed her wrist and with a sharp twist forced her to drop the weapon.

She screamed at him, "You bastard, you stinking son-of-a-bitch. Get away from me."

Then he pushed her back flat to the ground again, retrieved his knife and raised it in readiness to plunge into her chest. She closed her eyes, prepared to die, almost hoping for death to end the terror. Instead, she felt the hammer against her jaw, and, again, above her eyes. It was all hazy after that. She felt an excruciating stab of pain on one nipple. She was vaguely aware when his naked body covered hers and, more so, when he entered her. His rhythm was fast and urgent, and it was over quickly. He pulled away and got up. It was all a fog now, and she did not see him dress and walk away, leaving her bleeding and naked in the dust, baking in the sun at high noon.

She faded from consciousness until she felt something brushing against her sore breast. She stiffened, and it stopped. She sensed water on her lips and something lifting her head as her canteen pressed against her lips. She accepted a small drink of cool water and opened her eyes. The other Apache was kneeling beside her. She saw soft, dark eyes and felt no fear for some reason. He helped her sit up. He pointed to a little leather bag in one hand, then poured a bit of brown powder from it onto his hand and added a bit of water to make a paste which he applied to the bruising above her eye, which was nearly closed by the swelling. She looked down at her throbbing breast, strangely unembarrassed by her nakedness, though she wondered if this man had arrived for his turn at the woman.

She saw that the paste covered a ghastly wound where one nipple had been removed. She bit her lower lip and fought back tears, which she refused to surrender at the sight of the mutilation.

"Me Moon Watcher," the Apache said, his voice as soft and soothing as his eyes. He nodded at the little bag. "This help hurts. If want to live, obey El Gato." He stood and walked away.

Tabitha drank more from the canteen Moon Watcher had left. She slipped back into her moccasins and gathered up her clothes, including the tattered undergarments, and staggered to the blanket she had laid out earlier. There was the refuge of shade here, anyway. She dropped everything in a heap next to the blanket and collapsed into its soft embrace and fell asleep.

Some hours later, she awakened to the weight pressed against her body. She did not open her eyes, feigning sleep, not wanting to give him the satisfaction of either acceptance or resistance. She could feel the roughness of his shirt against her, stinging her injured breast. She could feel his breechclout against her thighs, so she assumed he had not bothered to disrobe but had just freed his male parts to be serviced. Again, it was over in seconds.

When he got to his feet, he said, "El Gato's woman. Eat."

He dropped something beside her on the blanket and walked away. She realized then she had not fooled him by playing possum. She remembered Moon Watcher's admonishment to obey El Gato. She decided that if she still chose to live, the Apache's words were good advice. She would obey but never surrender. Someday she would escape, but she had to survive to do that. She looked down at the clump of something El Gato had left on the blanket. Her first meal of the day. She picked it up. The same rancid crap they had been eating. She devoured it and washed it down with water.

Chapter 12

CAL RIVERS WONDERED when Manuelito was going to call off the hunt for the Apache war party. Almost ten days out, and they had not picked up a sign. The loose sand and dirt that frosted the surface of the land that tried to pass for grazing acres appeared to be swept clean. The cause was no doubt the intermittent blasts of dry wind that gusted randomly and rolled across the expanse, sometimes kicking up little whirlwinds of dust.

It was well before sunset when Manuelito signaled a stop at a stream of water that snaked through the prairie-desert from the low mountains and hill country to the north. When all had reined in their horses, he spoke at some length in Navajo. The riders began to dismount and lead their mounts along the edge of the stream to drink.

North Star remained with Cal and interpreted. "Manuelito says we are to turn back. Two will go on to try to locate the Mimbreno hideaway, probably in the mountains near the Mexican border. They will organize a larger war party and come back this way, heading for a place called Mushroom Rock to wait for word. He thinks we are too many to surprise and too few to succeed, since the Apaches have probably reached their village by now."

"Makes sense. I think we need to head back to the Hawk village anyhow. I went off and left Little Sis there, and she might want to be moving on. She ain't much for waiting on folks." He grinned and winked. "You might like to talk to that Still Water gal some more, I expect."

North Star flushed and shrugged. "Manuelito says we should spend the night at this place and leave at sunrise. Delgado wishes to seek his wife and son, so he will try to find where the captives were taken. Sundog will go with him."

"That little guy? He's not much more than a kid."

"He has seen twenty winters, Delgado told me. He may be small of stature, but he is a good tracker. He has a reputation for shrewdness, and he is light as an eagle's feather, so he rides like the wind. He will bring the news if the Apache stronghold is found."

They set up camp but still chose not to light fires in the unlikely event they were within sight of the Apaches. After laying out bedrolls, with still an hour of daylight remaining, the searchers dug into the meager remains of the food supplies. They scattered about the area in conversation clusters. Cal and North Star were joined by Delgado and Sundog. They gnawed on deer jerky and ate the last of a Navajo bread that Cal thought was still tasty, though quite dried-out and crusty. Cal took a swig from his canteen to wash down the skimpy fare, and his eyes caught sight of a little cloud of dust moving their direction.

At first, he thought it was one of the whirlwinds that had been skipping over the landscape during the day's ride, but its aim was too perfect as it shot directly toward the camp. Reflexively, his fingers touched the butt of his holstered Peacemaker. "I think we've got company," he said. "But I wouldn't look for trouble from a single rider heading into a war party."

The others turned their heads and looked toward the figure Cal had detected. The hazy outline of a man astride a paint horse came into view now.

Delgado said, "That is Nez. He rides his big paint stallion. Good horse."

As Nez neared the camp, Delgado and Sundog stood and waved him their way. Except for Manuelito, the other Navajo warriors remained where they were, all eyes watching the guest's arrival with mild curiosity. Manuelito got up and walked over to speak with Delgado. Cal and North Star stood when the leader approached.

"You know this man?" Manuelito asked. Cal assumed the chief was speaking English for his benefit.

Delgado replied. "It is Nez from our Hawk clan."

Manuelito nodded, "I remember Nez. He fought with the last resisters. Good man. Brave warrior."

When the rider arrived and dismounted, Cal recognized him. They had not been previously introduced, but he had observed the one-eared man at the village. Nez led his horse directly to Manuelito, disregarding the others, which Cal guessed was proper etiquette. They spoke rapidly in Navajo, or so it seemed to Cal, admitting that any language but English seemed to be spoken in double-time. He became concerned when he noticed the grim expression on North Star's face.

When Manuelito and Nez finished their dialogue, Cal asked North Star, "What is it?"

"Tabby has been taken."

"Taken? What do you mean?"

"Tabby and Still Water were attacked by Apaches at a place called Dripping Springs on their return from a trip to Fort Defiance. Still Water was shot but made it back to the village. She sent Nez to tell us. Nez says Still Water will recover, but she believes Tabby was abducted. She does not know if Tabby was injured. Others from the clan went to make a search of the canyon at Dripping Springs to be certain she was not killed, but Still Water thinks not."

Cal felt a sinking feeling in his gut before the pangs of self-blame set in. He never should have left her. Apaches. Tabby had survived Comanche abduction. Twice, in fact. She had lived almost a year with Quanah's Kwahadi band. But then she had been under the protection of She Who Speaks, now their sister-in-law, Jael Chernik Rivers. Five years before that she had escaped Comanche abduction when she was taken the day their mother and brother Josh's wife, Cassie, were killed by Comanche raiders at the Slash R Ranch. On that occasion, as a young teenager, she had raced from the war party's camp and disappeared into the river, swimming upstream and finally emerging to race miles before she met up with the rescue party. He prayed that her luck had not run out.

He saw that the others were looking at him expectantly. "I guess I would like to ride with Delgado and Sundog.

If Tabby's alive, she's going to end up in the same village as the others. But I need to get word to my family. God, this is going to kill Pop when he hears it. Tabby's his baby and his pet. But they've got to start preparing for the worst."

Delgado said, "Do this. Go to Fort Defiance and send a message over the talking wires to your people. The Army must be told about this. They will do more for a white captive than a Navajo. Still Water said your sister is known among your people."

"I hadn't thought about that, but I suppose there's something to it. She's wrote some books that sort of made her half-famous, I guess. Never read them myself. Pissed her some, I think. Just ain't much of a reader."

"I will go with you. My mother will never forgive me if something happens to my Aunt Summer's only child," North Star said.

Delgado said, "This journey will not end in a week or even a month. It will take great patience to find the renegade Mimbres band. And when we do, we must still wait to bring about the release of the prisoners, if they are alive and with the Apaches. You go to the fort and do what you must. Whenever you can, go to a place called Mushroom Rock. If we are not there, wait for us. That is where we meet. There is water and shelter, and it is on the American side of the border."

"How do I find this place? Hell, I don't know how to find Fort Defiance."

Nez broke in, "English no good." He began to sign as he spoke, one foreign language Cal spoke and understood proficiently. "Me take fort. Talk Chee Dodge. Know Mushroom Rock."

From the signing, Cal gathered that Dodge was an interpreter who also knew the country, and that between the interpreter and Nez, they would be able to give him good directions to the landmark. "How far to the fort?"

North Star translated to Nez in Navajo. The warrior replied. North Star said, "Six or seven days. He says it is about two days southwest of the Hawk clan village. We're about on the border between New Mexico and Arizona territories and the Mexican border's about three more days south of us."

"Shit. Time's wasting," Cal groaned.

"We have time," Delgado reminded. "There is no choice. Perhaps North Star could join Manuelito and the warriors who return to the village and confirm that the search has been made. Somebody can go with him to Fort Defiance, which would take another two days, and you can meet up there."

"I don't think North Star would mind that little detour none. Yeah, let's do what you say. Before we leave tomorrow, let me know what supplies I can pick up there. Maybe North Star can get our pack mule at the Hawk village, and we can get provisioned up some."

Manuelito finally spoke again. "It is decided. And when you find the Apache village, have your clan send for me. I will bring many warriors. They must learn to let the Diné live in peace, or there will be a heavy price. If one Diné dies, three Apaches die. Maybe more. Enough of this."

Chapter 13

JOSH RIVERS COULD not believe it. Not again. Tabby dancing with death, perhaps her last waltz. What in blazes had possessed her to go racing off on her latest adventure? She had it all, including a talented man who loved her and with whom she shared a beautiful new casa. The success of her books had secured her financial and literary future. She was truly an independent woman, but with that, in his mind, came responsibility to make wise choices. Damn. He loved his little sister. And he was terrified for her fate. And angry at her, too.

Clutching the telegram in his hand, he reached for his cane, wincing as he stood up. He walked down the hallway of the Rivers and Sinclair offices until he reached his junior partner's office. The oak door had the words "Jael Chernik Rivers" inscribed on it. The heavy door was ajar, so she was not consulting with a client. He tapped softly on the door before pushing it open.

"Need to talk," he said as he stepped into the austere office that was just starting to be nested following his wife's recent transfer from the firm's Fort Sill office.

Jael looked up from her desk and smiled, brushing back her sable mane before she spoke. "Why are you so grim? Was I too playful last night? You didn't seem to object." She paused. "Not in a mood for levity, huh? Okay, what's stuck in your craw?"

Josh sat down in front of Jael's desk, flipped the telegram across the desktop and waited for her to read it. Damn, she was a stunning creature. He still marveled at how tragedy closed one door in his life and ultimately opened another when he met this Jewish woman the Comanche had known as She Who Speaks in Quanah's village. And she had been mothering his abducted son for over four years. Fate? He had given up trying to reconcile the odds.

Jael was no longer smiling when she put the telegram down. "Cal doesn't say much. I guess a telegram doesn't allow for it. But Tabby's been taken by an Apache named El Gato. He's waiting at Fort Defiance for a reply before he takes up the search, I gather."

"I've got to hire a courier to let Pop and Nate know. I'll wire Ham in Denver. I'll head out to Fort Defiance tomorrow."

"No, you will not," she declared adamantly. "We're still bringing the buggy the two miles to town with you groaning all the way."

"That's not fair. I don't complain that much."

"No, but I can tell you're hurting. It hasn't even been three weeks since you took that bullet in the thigh, and the doctor said the wound's a slow healer. You can't be sitting on a horse for a trip like that. Be honest with yourself."

Josh shrugged. "I feel I've got to be doing something."

"Yes. Your legal work. Danna says you're not close to caught up from your last absence, and she needs your help on the Castro land grant case. There is serious money for the firm there if we're successful. I am going to ride out and let Oliver know about this. It's not far from noon. Let's grab a bite to eat at the Exchange Hotel and then I'll go talk to him."

"You know he will be in the saddle and on his way to Fort Defiance tomorrow morning."

"And I will be riding out with him."

He had feared this. Tabby was Jael's closest female friend. "Please, don't do this, Jael. You can't help out there."

"Not tough enough? I haven't always worn these horrible frilly things so-called civilized ladies wear. You do recall I lived more than seven years among the Comanche? I can outshoot most men with a Winchester."

He knew he was fighting a losing battle, and he did not want her to leave angry. "Do you think it is appropriate for a woman to accompany a man unchaperoned across New Mexico Territory?"

"You don't trust me?"

"Of course, I trust you. I was thinking of appearances."

"Most folks know you married a savage. It will give the church ladies something to chatter about. Besides, I do speak some Apache. That might be useful."

"You do? You never mentioned that."

"I'm not fluent. But I can still converse reasonably well if I toss in some signs. We held two captured Apache women with the Kwahadi band, and Quanah asked me to communicate with them. It was fun because it gave me a chance to learn another language. The young one became a warrior's third wife, and I helped her learn Comanche. The older was past child-bearing age and was traded back to the Apaches for a pretty, young Mexican woman who had young bucks fighting to claim her as a wife."

"I don't like it, but I surrender."

"I will see that you have a pleasant goodbye tonight. I promise I will not hurt you."

"You are a wicked woman."

AS JAEL HAD predicted, Oliver Wolf, a mixed-blood Cherokee formerly known as White Wolf, started making plans for the journey to Fort Defiance the instant she informed him of his lover's dilemma. An artist, whose work was increasingly in demand and the proprietor of a busy construction operation, Wolf's absence would no doubt cost him dearly in lost commissions.

They were sitting in the large parlor of the Spanish-style home Wolf had designed and built with the assistance of craftsmen from Wolf Builders. Wolf passed the telegram back to Jael. "I will need to make some arrangements, but I will leave in the morning. With a spare mount, I can reach Fort Defiance in three days taking the Albuquerque route, bypassing most of the mountain and hill country. Pablo already handles the day-to-day work of the construction business, and I just need to let him know. The paintings will wait, but I must arrange for someone to notify the purchasers of the delay. The Laurent family will be living in this house for at least several more months. Angelina is busy with the new baby, but her stepdaughter, Margo, has been looking after the house and would probably make client contacts for me. She has been cataloguing and naming my projects."

"I can ask Rylee to see to the horses."

"I am certain Gabriel would do that for me before and after he goes to work at your law offices."

Josh and Jael resided within easy walking distance of Wolf's home, and their foster daughter, Rylee O'Brian, a bank officer at the tender age of eighteen, shared their home. Gabriel Laurent, a law clerk studying law in the Rivers firm, temporarily lived in Wolf's home with his sister and stepmother pending their return to a hacienda in the mountains north of Santa Fe.

Jael said, "I have a hunch Rylee and Gabriel will be sharing chore duty."

Wolf surrendered a wry smile. "Yes, and I suspect chores will take a fair amount of time. I hope things work out for them and that they will be patient. It is best to become friends first, is it not? Romance can come later. But who am I to dispense wisdom? It did not work out so well for me, did it?"

"Your story is not finished, Oliver. There are many chapters to be written. By the way, I am going with you."

He shot her an incredulous look. "I must have misunderstood. I thought you said you were going with me."

"Yes. I speak some Apache, and you know I can take care of myself. Tabby's my best friend, and Josh isn't in any condition to travel."

"And Josh doesn't object?"

"I wouldn't say that. But he won't stand in my way. You may recall the situation was reversed a month back."

"Yes, and Josh's trip with me to the Laurent hacienda did not work out so well."

"I don't plan on getting shot."

"Nobody does, but it still happens."

"I'll pack five days of food supplies and bring an Army pup tent and bedroll. I'll talk Josh out of his buckskin gelding and bring my mare as an extra mount. We won't have a lot of gear, but a packhorse might be handy."

"Yes. That would give us another spare mount, too, in case a horse comes up lame. I will bring a packhorse over to your house a half-hour after sunrise and help you load the supplies."

Jael stood to leave, and Wolf got up and followed her to the door. She turned and reached out and gave him a hug. "We'll find her, Oliver, and bring her back here where she belongs."

"Yes, we will find her. Whether she chooses to return here remains to be seen."

Chapter 14

TABITHA HAD LOST track of time during the days since her capture by El Gato and Moon Watcher, but she thought about two weeks had passed. The Apaches took twisted trails that led into the foothills and then back onto terrain that was near desert, followed by journeys into the foothills again. She could have sworn they sometimes passed the same location twice. She could make no sense of their meandering unless her captors were trying to lay false trails for possible pursuers. She thought pursuit was pure conjecture, although she supposed others knew of her disappearance by now.

She had concluded that El Gato had claimed her as a wife. He had taken her daily since that first assault, sometimes returning for seconds. She became a rag doll at those times, compliant but unresponsive. She supposed she had become something of a whore, purchasing survival with her naked body. Yes, she would be his damned wife until she could make herself his widow.

El Gato never lay with her after he finished, probably knowing he slept beside her at the risk of his life. She would kill him if she could reach a weapon—his knife, a stone, or whatever implement of death might be within reach. Beyond the conjugal visits from El Gato, he rarely spoke to her now, and she communicated mostly with Moon Watcher, who treated her with surprising consideration and spoke a smattering more English than El Gato. It was made clear she was expected to do a squaw's chores now. Build a fire when it was deemed safe to do so. Skin and gut the occasional rabbit or rattlesnake they killed and roast the meat over the flames. She had done such things during her life with the Comanche, and she thought El Gato was pleased when he saw she was competent in carrying out such tasks. But, of course, he would never offer more than a grunt and usually found some fault. Regardless, she had followed Moon Watcher's admonition to obey and had avoided further beatings. The wound on her breast was starting to heal, and an amputated nipple was the least of her worries, as she saw it.

They were headed back into the foothills now, and mid-morning El Gato reined his stallion into a grove of scraggly pines, and they followed a narrow deer path that weaved through the trees. The prickly branches whipped her face and neck as the warrior broke through the thick undergrowth oblivious to the woman who trailed him. She lowered her head and focused on warding off the wicked needles with her free arm. Not soon enough for Tabitha, they broke free of the trees and rode out onto an established trail that appeared to lead higher into the foothills and the low mountains beyond. She wondered if they had crossed the Mexican border.

By early afternoon the trail twisted into the mountains, and the riders moved snail-like on a ledge that made a trail along a jagged stone wall that descended several hundred feet below the path, the depth increasing with each step further up the steep incline. Tabitha averted her eyes from the abyss and focused on the precipitous ascent ahead.

As they approached the summit, Tabitha caught sight of an Apache warrior standing on an overhang that jutted off the wall and widened the trail for a short distance. He was attired in cotton Mexican garb, his trouser legs tucked into the calf-high moccasins Apaches seemed to favor, and he had a rifle cradled in his arms. He raised a hand in greeting to El Gato, and the chief reined his mount to a halt. The men spoke for a few moments. El Gato nodded and then kneed his big calico stallion ahead.

Less than a half-hour later, the trail started to level off, and they rode onto a stone-littered mesa that Tabitha estimated might extend south for a mile or more but would be less than a half-mile east to west at most places. Wood-framed wickiups, many covered with tree branches, shrubbery, and grass, others with hides or even canvas, dotted the stark landscape. Some had brush arbors in front of or adjacent to the living structure offering shade or shelter for those working outside, or, perhaps, for social gatherings.

The mesa on the east had no barrier but appeared to drop off suddenly over sheer cliffs that would thwart any enemy. To the west, a precipice reaching to the mountaintop above overlooked the mesa and guarded against invaders. It would be nearly impossible for enemies to attack from the direction they had entered, she figured, but there must be at least one other outlet from the mountain fortress. She intended to make it her business to find it.

Their arrival at the village had not gone unnoticed, and as they rode into the clusters of wickiups, occupants began to gather. El Gato and Moon Watcher dismounted, and a pretty young woman wearing a doeskin dress and resting a baby on her hip slipped from the crowd of greeters and came up to Moon Watcher, raised her hand, and pressed it against the warrior's uplifted hand. He smiled at the woman and surrendered a brief adoring look at the baby, whom Tabitha guessed was a girl child. Moon Watcher's wife and child, she assumed.

Still astride Socks, Tabitha realized she was now becoming the focus of a horde of curious onlookers. Small children had assembled around her, looking up with wide eyes, a few of the girls offering friendly smiles but most of the boys sober-faced and reserving judgment. She supposed they required some signal from the adults before deciding whether the stranger was friend or foe.

Tabitha noted that the gathering consisted mostly of women with a sprinkling of elderly men, suggesting that most of the warriors not taking up sentry duty were away from the village hunting or raiding. It occurred to her then that there were only a few horses staked out on the mesa, meaning that the herd was secured elsewhere, but within a short distance, of course. No warrior of the Southwestern tribes would fall asleep at night without his horse nearby. She added finding the location of the remuda to her mental list of tasks.

El Gato was speaking to the assemblage now, gesturing toward Tabitha, but she had not a clue about what he was saying. She saw Moon Watcher discreetly leading his horse away, accompanied by his presumed wife and child. This made her uneasy, since the presence of the warrior had given her a strange sense of comfort that contrasted to the unpredictability of the volatile El Gato.

Another woman, tall and long-limbed, broke from the crowd, stepped up to El Gato and began speaking rapidly, the tone of her voice angry and insolent. She was not classically beautiful, but her angular features and flawless skin gave her an exotic handsomeness, Tabitha thought. El Gato listened with uncharacteristic patience before he finally spoke sharply to the woman. At the same moment his hand swung around and struck her face, almost knocking her off her feet. He pointed to the wickiups and issued an obvious order to leave. The woman shot arrows with the flash of her eyes when she looked up at Tabitha before she whirled and stomped away. The observers had stopped their chatter and begun to break up and return to whatever they were doing before El Gato appeared with his trophy.

El Gato turned back to Tabitha. "Down," he ordered.

She could see this was not a time to question, so she obeyed and dismounted, almost wishing for the routine of recent days again. He walked over to the stockinged gelding and yanked the Henry rifle from its scabbard. She reached to pull it from his hands. "Mine," she said.

"Mine," he replied backhanding her and catching the bridge of her nose. He pointed to the horse. "Mine."

Tabitha staggered backward at the blow, the stinging of her nose almost launching her into a rage that would have sent her in a futile, possibly dangerous, attack on the Apache. Instead, she righted herself and stood there seething.

He untied the blanket that was rolled up behind the saddle and tossed it to her. Then El Gato called to a boy who looked to be twelve or thirteen years old and was sitting in front of the nearest wickiup, honing a length of unidentifiable animal's leg bone with a flint rock, probably fashioning a weapon of some sort, she assumed. The boy immediately abandoned his project and ran to the chief, who handed him the reins of their horses and issued another of his orders. She had observed that the man never seemed to ask for anything. He demanded or ordered. She was struck by a sense of emptiness when she saw her new friend Socks being led away. Thank God, Smokey had been too lame to ride to this place.

"Follow," El Gato said.

She trailed behind him, as he led her through the maze of wickiups located on the near end of the village. He stopped where the woman who had greeted Moon Watcher was working over a fire and spoke to her in a soft and gentle manner. Evidently, he was expected to treat his friend's wife with respect. She heard El Gato say "Ta-Bee" and concluded she was the topic of conversation. The woman nodded and stood up and looked at Tabitha, showing traces of a friendly smile and kind eyes that offered empathy. Instantly, she felt safer somehow.

El Gato walked away and left her with the Apache woman, who Tabitha guessed was in her mid-twenties, about her own age. Now what?

"My name Walks Far. And you Ta-Bee?"

Tabitha was shocked and excited to hear the woman speak English. How sweet the sound. "Yes, Ta-Bee is fine. I did not expect to hear you speak English."

"Not so good, maybe, but can make talk with you. I learned at white school at fort during Long Walk."

"You were on the Long Walk? How can that be?"

"I am Diné. Always Diné. I was taken by Apaches at Bosque Redondo almost one-half my life ago when in my thirteenth summer. Now, this my home. My husband. My children. Maybe before I die can see Diné family again."

"It is 1879. We will see many changes over ten to twenty years' time. You will see your Diné family again, perhaps sooner than you think. I am certain of it."

"That my hope. Now, Ta-Bee come with me."

Walks Far led Tabitha deeper into the village and stopped in front of a sagging and tattered wickiup that was begging for repair. "Cold Wind and wives sleep here. Go back to San Carlos with babies. Want safe life. Ta-Bee sleep here."

Tabitha pulled back a deerskin flap that covered the opening and peered inside. In the dusky interior she could make out a small stone-edged fire pit in the center, and the smoke hole in the ceiling above that allowed a hazy beam of light to enter. It was a pitiful shelter but an improvement over the open sky she had slept under the past several weeks, especially if it took a notion to rain. Perhaps she could do some repairs if this was to be her residence during what she considered her temporary stay.

As if reading her mind, Walks Far said, "I help Ta-Bee fix lodge when sun come again. Follows No Man help, too."

"Follows No Man?"

"Son. Eight summers."

Tabitha tossed her skinny bedroll in the wickiup. "You will have to tell me what is expected of me."

"I bring old buffalo robe and Mexican blanket. Eat with us night come. El Gato not see you this night, maybe not next. Makes peace with Cactus Bloom." Walks Far smiled and giggled at this.

"That was the woman he fought with?"

"Wife. Not want more wife for husband."

"You mean me? I am El Gato's wife?"

"Number two wife. Cactus Bloom be boss wife."

"Will I share their wickiup?"

"I think no. Cactus Bloom not want. She make El Gato sorry Ta-Bee sleep there. Ta-Bee stay here, I think. She never like Ta-Bee, but I am friend."

"I am grateful to find a friend here." Her start in the Apache village was not as terrible as she had anticipated. She was prepared for the worst in the days ahead. But it eased her mind to have someone who was at least marginally fluent in English nearby, and it was a relief that she would not likely be sharing a lodge with Cactus Bloom anytime soon.

Chapter 15

WITH WALKS FAR'S help, Tabitha found herself becoming accustomed to living in the Apache stronghold. Her experience among the Comanche served her well. She had known near starvation and total deprivation in the weeks before Quanah's surrender and during the trek to the reservation at Fort Sill. Here, there seemed to be ample food, for now anyway. She noticed they had been eating more beef than wild game since her arrival and that corn and wheat and other grains were ground on stones and converted to flours used to make assorted breads. She was surprised to find fruits occasionally poured from commercial cans. She assumed that most of their food supply was the result of raids on farms and ranches, probably many in Mexico. There were more than a few fresh blood-crusted scalps suspended from warriors' lances and hanging on braided deer hide strips outside wickiup entryways.

She felt sad for the Mexican people. Their government, as with most she had observed, followed the doctrine of unintended consequences in its rush to respond to public outcry. In an effort to eradicate the Apaches who raided from the north, El Presidente had declared that a bounty would be offered for each Apache scalp. The problem: who could distinguish an Apache scalp from a Mexican's? Several critics claimed that far more Mexican scalps than those of Apaches were being turned in by the bounty hunters. Even some Apaches were said to be marketing Mexican scalps through the traders who dealt with the bands.

She had been in the camp two weeks and her presence was accepted now. There seemed to be little concern about her fleeing. Where would she go? But she was taking note of village routines and the layout of her surroundings, storing information for when it might be useful.

Much of the time she was no more than Cactus Bloom's servant, gathering wood, scraping skins, and collecting water in buffalo or cow paunches, clay or woven containers, and a few tin buckets. The water source was a stream that ran along the west edge of the village. The fast-rushing stream descended from the mountainside, slicing through the mesa before disappearing down the canyon that sloped away from the south side of the village. She did not mind fetching the water because it took her away from Cactus Bloom's watchful eye and gave her opportunities to explore her surroundings.

Cactus Bloom often beat her with a stick for perceived failures that Tabitha did not understand. The blows stung but were endurable. She had learned to dodge and offer her backside and shoulders as the best targets for her punishment. The number one wife spoke little or no English, and Tabitha was just starting to grasp a few Apache words, so communication was difficult.

Cactus Bloom had two daughters, nine-year old Little Bloom and five-year old Quiet Mouse. The older girl had little to do with Tabitha, but the younger girl seemed taken with her, and followed her as she carried out her tasks. Cactus Bloom seemed happy enough to have her daughter out from underfoot. The girl was shy with most of the villagers, but Tabitha enjoyed breaking her shell and slowly was picking up Apache words from her and teaching her a few English words. They both had fun making a game of it.

This evening, she sat outside her wickiup, needle and sinew in hand, trying to repair the tattered buckskins she had worn into the camp. She expected to wear them again one day, along with the new moccasins she was making. The few dresses she had been given by Walks Far were of Mexican origin and not suitable for riding.

"Sit with you?"

Tabitha looked up and saw Walks Far, who had approached silently as was her way, with the baby, Peace Searcher, in her arms. They often talked before darkness set in, especially when the men were absent. All but a handful of warriors had left on a raiding or hunting party this morning. They were expected to be gone a week or more. Tabitha was delighted to be free of El Gato's nocturnal visits for a spell. "Of course, please join me. You are always welcome here, my friend."

Walks Far sat down beside Tabitha, slipped one side of her doeskin dress down over her shoulder, exposing her engorged breast and offering a nipple to the baby girl who latched on eagerly. "Ta-Bee not stay," Walks Far said matter-of-factly. "Die maybe if run. El Gato find. I be sad."

"I will leave if given a chance. But I do not know when that will happen. I do not want to die. But I will not live my life out among the Apache."

"I talk to Sunrise. She say Diné go with you."

Sunrise was Delgado's wife. She had been taken as a second or third wife for the warrior One Hand and spoke

English. She had sought out Tabitha when they were filling water containers at the stream a week earlier. Tabitha had learned that all the captive Navajos were still being held in the village. Sunrise, of course, had not known that Tabitha had met her husband, Delgado, and had been thrilled to learn that a search was being made. Tabitha had not had the heart to tell the woman that the search had no doubt been abandoned by now—at least by all but Cal and Delgado. Only death would stop Cal's search. She was certain of that. She responded to Walks Far's comment. "I promised Sunrise I would not leave without the other captives. Have you told Moon Watcher of our plans?"

"No do that. Always Diné. Husband no hurt, if no tell. Want peace. Moon Watcher want peace. No peace with El Gato. No peace with Victorio. I want to go San Carlos. Peace there. Hope there."

"If you go to San Carlos, I promise I will find you there someday. You will always be my friend."

Walks Far smiled wanly, "Hope for that."

They talked for more than an hour before Walks Far left to find her boy, Follow No Man. During their conversation, Tabitha learned that Walks Far had lost a middle child during an attack by soldiers on their village before the survivors were herded to the reservation two years earlier. Moon Watcher's friendship with El Gato since boyhood and his simmering hate for the white soldiers resulting from his son's violent death had motivated him to take his family and jump the reservation with El Gato's band. Now he was having second thoughts.

Tabitha and Walks Far also talked about what the Navajo woman remembered of the Long Walk and agreed they would talk more of it another time. Tabitha admitted to herself that she had a selfish motive for searching out a pre-pubescent girl's perspective of what happened to the Diné during that wretched time.

Later, as Tabitha lay on her soft robe, cocooned in her blankets to escape the chill of the night air, she was grateful again that El Gato would not this night crawl naked into her robe and blankets to confirm his claim on her. She never knew when he might appear. Not every night, but most. She supposed some nights he took both wives. He never fell asleep beside her. Enjoyed her once, sometimes twice, and left. She suspected there would be hell to pay if he did not spend most of the night with Cactus Bloom.

She turned her mind to something that was deeply troubling her now. She and Oliver Wolf had made crazy and passionate love countless times for more than a year before she last shared his bed nearly seven weeks ago.

Safe contraceptives were almost impossible to obtain since passage by Congress of the Comstock Act of 1873 that had declared devices such as condoms obscene and illegal. She knew what caused babies and had accepted the risk. She had not become pregnant. Part of her would have loved to bear Oliver's child, but she had preferred to remain childless—at least for some years. There were too many interesting and exciting things to do with a life that offered so many trade-offs.

But she had missed her monthly a week earlier, and she had always been regular. She tried to convince herself the turmoil that had entered her life was the cause. She had been told many times that such things could affect the menstrual period. However, God forbid, if she were with child, it could not be Oliver's.

Chapter 16

CAL ASKED EUSTIS Cramb, one of the liverymen at the civilian stable just outside of Fort Defiance, to send a message to his campsite near the spring upon arrival of Oliver Wolf and Jael Rivers. He had expected the riders yesterday and hoped they had not run into trouble along the trail. He reminded himself that the man he had known as White Wolf would never abuse his horses. If a mount was due for rest, Wolf would call a halt, deadline be damned.

Cal sat on a stump, whittling on a forked stick that he intended to fashion into a roasting implement, although he had nothing available to roast. Noon dinner would probably be a steak served at the tavern. He had agreed to meet North Star at Ollie's Place, which had no restrictions on serving Indians.

They would both pass up the booze in favor of sarsaparilla. North Star had successfully warded off the alcohol curse that killed his father, and Cal was fighting to wean himself from the bottle, closing in on a month's success now. He was thinking clearly these days and plotting strategies to be a presence in the lives of his small children, unsure yet if he cared about winning back Erin McKenna Rivers, his estranged wife. She was a wealthy ranch heiress, red-haired, bright, and beautiful, and head honcho of the Circle M operation in northeastern New Mexico. He knew he could not live with her as a kept man.

He kicked his personal problems out of his thoughts. Tabby had to be his only concern for now. Recovery of his little sister had become an obsession, and he had decided to allow Wolf and Jael one more day. If they had not shown up by tomorrow, he and North Star would head out to meet up with Delgado and Sundog at the place called Mushroom Rock. The destination was a four- or five-day journey from Fort Defiance, according to Chee Dodge.

North Star was waiting for him when he walked into the saloon-café with a white-washed clapboard front and canvas-covered interior. The walls were mostly rolled up today to allow the breath of a dry wind to creep in and circulate to help nullify the hot sun rays that were beating down on the fragile ceiling. Cal pulled out a chair at a table furthest from the bar that his friend had chosen. A few enlisted men sat at a table near the bar, which was fashioned from three sawhorses and some long planks. Behind the crude bar were several tiers of shelving constructed from old crates on which were lined bottles of varying shapes and sizes containing the fluids from which the business prospered.

The cooking was done out back, possibly to reduce fire risk, Cal assumed. Or, perhaps, diners would prefer to remain ignorant of the food preparation process. It didn't matter to Cal. The grub was edible, and it beat his own cooking, which he would be doing soon enough when they hit the trail again.

North Star pushed a bottle of sarsaparilla across the table to him. "Ordered this for you. It was not going to be any cooler sitting on a shelf behind the bar than here on the table."

"Nothing like warm sarsaparilla."

"No word on your sister-in-law or this Oliver Wolf yet?"

"Nope. They got till tomorrow noon, and then we're riding out."

"Man built like a cougar with an extra layer of muscle just walked in. Mixed-blood, I'd guess. Gentleman sort. He held the door open for a lady dressed in snug buckskins, moccasins and a low-crowned hat. They look fresh off the trail, but this woman would turn any man's head. I don't think she could make herself ugly if she tried."

"Wolf and Jael." Cal swung around, waved, and stood up. North Star joined him.

Wolf and Jael walked toward them, sharing sober faces. When Jael reached Cal, she gave him a hug and held him tight for a moment. Then she turned to North Star and extended her hand while Wolf and Cal exchanged greetings.

"I am Jael Rivers," she said, "Tabby's friend and sister-in-law."

"I am her cousin, North Star. I am pleased to meet you. Tabby has spoken of you often."

Wolf stepped over and introduced himself to North Star, taking his hand in a firm grip. "Oliver Wolf, North Star. Call me Wolf. Polite society in Santa Fe and a few family members call me Oliver, but that's a made-up name."

"Tabby has told me of your history. She is very proud of you and your work. I am glad you have joined us," North Star replied.

They all sat down at the table, and the young, fuzzy-cheeked bartender, who doubled as a waiter for the few occupants, approached the table. "Something to drink for the newcomers?"

"Sarsaparilla," Wolf said.

"Two beers," Jael said.

The bartender was struck speechless for a moment. Cal figured serving a woman in the saloon might be a first for him, and there would certainly have been no precedent for selling alcohol to a female. He decided to help the young man. "Everything's on me," he said. "I enjoyed a bit of a windfall during my journey to visit the Diné. We need to order dinner. These folks must be starving, just off the trail. Today's special for everybody."

After the bartender left, Cal explained to Jael and Wolf, "Steak, fried potatoes, and pie is all they serve anytime. Kind of pie's a guess, but I'd bet apple. Dessert's the best part. I think some enlisted man's wife bakes the pies at the fort. Potatoes will be a little burnt and crusty. Steak will be okay but on the rare side. But if you say well done, you get a chunk of coal."

The bartender returned with the drinks, setting two foaming beer mugs on the table in front of Jael, who promptly picked one up and pressed it to her lips. She took a big swallow and grimaced. "Tastes like panther piss," she said before taking another swallow.

She downed her first beer quickly but did not touch the other. Cal figured she was saving it to drink with her meal. Damn, he would swear that full beer mug had a finger on it just coaxing him to try a sip. Of course, Jael would not be aware of his problem, and he told himself he had better get used to the temptation. North Star had told him it would always be there. And later, he would feel uplifted by another victory over the demon.

Jael asked, "Is there any news of Tabby?"

Cal said, "Nothing. We are supposed to meet two Navajo friends who are out scouting the country where Apache bands hide out. They're going to meet us at a place called Mushroom Rock, and their report will tell us what we do after that. We got directions to Mushroom Rock from an interpreter named Chee Dodge, so I'm sure I can find it. North Star just got back from the Hawk clan village. Manuelito—he's some kind of a big chief, they say—is putting together a bigger search party and they're going to head back south again."

North Star said, "He was going back to his own village first, so it will probably be four or five days before they strike out again. He wants to be in the vicinity to back us up if we find something. But we can't count on when they might show up or if we can make connections."

Wolf asked, "How many warriors are with this El Gato? Any idea?"

Cal said, "Forty to fifty, I'd guess. And most took their families with them when they jumped the reservation. There's more bad news. Word came to the fort three days back that Victorio has led more Mimbres Apaches—maybe twice as many—off the San Carlos reservation. I don't know if they will join up with El Gato's bunch, but if they do, it will take the Army to flush them out of the mountains. I think Tabby's in more danger if the Army mixes in. I'd like to get her out of there first. I don't know if she can be ransomed, but I got a stash of gold, and the bastards can have it all for my little sis."

Wolf said, "I don't understand how she was captured in the first place. Tell us how this all came about."

A Mexican girl from the outdoor kitchen brought a tray with their dinners and placed the plates on the table. Cal had been right. Apple pie. The steaks were charred, but the potatoes had not been damaged beyond recognition. He commenced telling his story while they ate. "It all started a few days after we met up with this strange woman and her addled son. She sold me a mule-load of furs, and North Star's lady friend and Tabby went to the fort to find a buyer."

"Stop," Wolf said. "Tell me about this lady friend and her son."

"Well, she was a tall woman, black hair, dark with scary eyes. Kind of put you under her spell. I don't know many men who could say no if she was to invite you to share her blanket . . . sorry, Jael."

Jael rolled her eyes. "Just tell us your tale, Cal."

"She was dressed like an old trapper. Claimed her husband died and left her and her son up in the mountains on their own. They was on the old Carson Trail headed for Albuquerque. Story didn't make no sense, but I agreed to take the furs off her hands. Tabby didn't trust the woman. She thought the poor lady was going to try to kill me when I was paying her for the furs and threatened to shoot her with that Henry of hers. We finished the deal, and Tabby ran them off. Hell, she was just a woman in need of help. She wasn't no robber. She rode this white stallion that would be close to a match for that black spooky stallion of yours." Cal called Wolf's stallion, Owl, spooky because of the white spectacle-like circles around the horse's eyes.

Wolf said, "The woman's name was Lilith. She murdered her husband and was responsible for the deaths of others. Josh and I were tracking her when Josh got shot by the woman's right-hand man. Josh took him down, but we had to turn back. But that's another story."

"Damn. Maybe Little Sis had the woman figured out after all."

Jael interrupted, "Cal, just tell us how El Gato entered the picture."

Between Cal and North Star, the two men related the story of the initial encounter with El Gato and what they knew of the journey Tabitha and Still Water made to Fort Defiance and back again to Dripping Springs where the attack and abduction took place.

Cal said, "They must have followed us to the Navajo lands. Doesn't make sense. One woman. Their war party already had a good number of captives. Why? If this El Gato is the head honcho, he should have been with his warriors."

Wolf said, "Some women can take a hold on a man. Drive them crazy. Scramble their brains." He gave a wry smile and nodded at Jael. "I speak from personal experience that Tabby can do that. Cal, your brother Josh married one of those."

Jael raised her eyebrows and gave Wolf a look of feigned exasperation.

"Anyway," Wolf continued, "El Gato must have seen Tabby someplace along the trail and become obsessed by her, decided he had to claim her. I can't come up with any other reason he would have followed her and stalked her the way he must have. From her standpoint, sitting where we are now, his motive works for her—and us."

"What do you mean?" Cal asked.

"She's quick as a whip's snap. Tabby will figure out what she's got to do to stay alive, and El Gato didn't go through all this trouble just to kill her. She's alive. I know she is, and she's likely plotting her own escape. That's what worries me most—that she will get killed trying to escape. We need to find out where she's at and get there before she makes a dangerous move."

Cal could not argue with Wolf's thinking. "More reason for us to move out quick-like."

Wolf said, "First thing in the morning, if that suits you. Jael and I have to do some shopping at the trading post this afternoon, and our horses need a good rest and feeding before they go back to work."

"I promised Major Richards, the post commandant, that I'd let him know when we was pulling out. The Army's got troops in the field, but they don't know where the hell they're going. I promised I'd get word back if we learned anything that would help."

"Only after Tabby's safe with us. The last thing we want is a troop of cavalry bursting into a village. There will always be some that will shoot anything that breathes—man, woman, or child. That's one reason I didn't renew my scouting enlistment for the Red River War. It got so I wasn't certain whether I was working for the good guys or the bad guys."

Cal replied, "I know what you're saying. But right now, I don't give a damn if I'm a good guy or a bad guy. I'm getting Little Sis back."

Chapter 17

WOLF HAD QUIETLY taken charge of the rescue party. There was no better scout and no better man to cover your back than Cal Rivers, but unlike some in the Rivers clan, including Tabitha, Cal seemed to feel no compulsion to lead. Jael would give Wolf plenty of rope until she disagreed but would not hesitate to challenge if she had misgivings about his decisions.

The searchers were making a bigger footprint on the semi-arid land than Wolf would have liked. Four riders, each with a spare mount, and two pack mules, one loaded with food and necessities for a long journey and the other packed with trade goods—clothing, blankets, pots and pans, foodstuffs and the like. Guns and alcohol had been intentionally omitted from the inventory.

Upon seeing the mule packed with trade goods, Cal had commented, "Didn't know this was a trading mission."

Wolf had simply replied, "Maybe, maybe not." The trade goods might be wasted. Of course, the Apaches could just take what they wanted and kill the merchants, but he thought it possible the cargo and a convincing story might open a door someplace. And he and Cal, between them, carried a small fortune in gold pieces for ransom. To some Indians, the gold meant nothing. Others realized the value of such coinage for purchase of guns and other supplies, including alcohol. Disclosure would need to be discreet, or the Apaches might just take the gold along with some scalps. Cal's blond hair would not bring a bounty in Mexico, but the others of their party bore marketable hair.

It was almost high noon of their fifth day out, and they were headed southeast, where Wolf could make out the faintest outline of shadowy mountain peaks against an azure backdrop in the distance. Cal had insisted they should be within a few hours of Mushroom Rock and had ridden ahead to make a scout. Wolf had no doubt his friend would find the place.

During his brief time in this godforsaken country, including some time with the Navajo search party, Cal

Rivers had not missed much. Wolf had found Cal to be a virtual encyclopedia when it came to survival here, instinctively knowing where to find water sources, hideaway canyons, and seldom-used trails. There was more to this man than his countrified demeanor would at first impression suggest. They had not scouted together during the Comanche wars, and Wolf's acquaintance with Cal had been brief and superficial, but Tabby had always maintained unwavering faith in the youngest of her four older brothers. "Do not ever underestimate, Cal," she had said often, "he just marches to the beat of his own drum."

Puffs of dust on the horizon warned Wolf that a rider was coming their way. Instinctively his fingers brushed the stock of the Winchester cradled in his rifle scabbard. It was likely Cal, but he would not relax until he confirmed it. He cast his eyes about and nodded approvingly when he saw North Star and Jael had joined his response. Moments later, he could make out the lanky frame of the tall rider headed at breakneck speed in their direction. Wolf signaled the others to rein in and await Cal's arrival.

When he pulled up in front of his comrades, Cal's grim face told Wolf his messenger was not carrying good news. "What is it?" Wolf asked.

"I found Mushroom Rock, and it looks like Delgado and Sundog are holed up there. Problem is they got company."

"Not friendly neighbors, I assume."

"Apaches. They was on the move, and I couldn't get a good count with the dust and all, but I'd guess seven, maybe eight, of the devils. Our guys are forted up in the rocks, but they ain't going no place. Apaches will work up to their position sooner or later and overrun them, I'm afraid."

"Tell me what their situation looks like."

"Well, they got their backs covered on the south by a sandstone wall that juts out of the ground from no place. Kind of round-topped and part of it sticks out over the front like a big umbrella. I guess somebody thought it looked like a big mushroom, but I can't make it look like one in my head. I suppose it could be climbed from the back, but it's a good thirty feet high and damned steep. It would take a spell. I sure as hell wouldn't try it. Better suited for a monkey. The thing runs about twenty feet long, so the south side ain't bad for protection. Big boulders scattered all over the north side, and somebody's rolled some into place to make a barricade before—likely been a lot of shoot-outs there between whites and Indians, Apaches and Navajos and whoever else was in a fighting mood."

"Is there any cover for us to move in from east and west without being seen? We don't want to risk coming from the north and firing south. We might hit one of our friends with a stray bullet."

"No cover up close enough to help. There's an arroyo not far west where we can stake out the spare horses and pack mules while we make a run at them."

Wolf had served as a young major in the First Cherokee Brigade with the Confederate Army and considered what he might have done during that time in such a situation. "We can change plans after we get nearer if we have to, but after we tie the extra animals, I'm thinking I would like to circle and move in from the south behind the outcropping. Then we'll split up, and Jael and I will come around from the east side of the mushroom and you and North Star from the west. If we can get that far without being spotted, we ought to be able to even the odds fast and avoid one of us going down in crossfire. Sometimes, I'd swear I've seen as many men shot by their own as by the enemy."

As they drew closer to the battle site, Wolf could hear sporadic gunfire and took that as a positive sign. Silence would have likely portended victory for the Apaches. They located the arroyo Cal had found and staked the horses and mules. There were sparse patches of brown grass among the yucca, sage and agave that claimed spots on the rough slopes, and Wolf figured that would keep the critters content for a spell.

As the gunfire grew louder, the riders moved toward a low ridge that overlooked the scene, and when they came over the rise and reined in their mounts, Wolf slipped his mariner's telescope from the sheath that was suspended from his saddle horn and focused on the action near the stone formation below. He quickly concluded the fighting was a standoff for the moment. Delgado and Sundog were well fortified in the rocks and could hold out for a spell. The Apaches could run the defenders over, however, if they were willing to risk the loss of three or four men. Pride would likely push them to make that attempt soon. They appeared to be grouping up their horses now to talk. Wolf guessed the warriors were debating abandonment of the attack or a semi-suicidal rush.

He turned to his comrades. "We'd better move. Let's ride behind the ridge till it feathers out and head south until we're out of sight range. Then we'll hook back and come up behind the mushroom formation. We'll split and join the fight when I raise my hand. Questions?"

Cal asked, "Are we trying to scare them off or should we take them all down?"

"Survivors would bring others to hunt for us and take revenge. No quarter."

As they approached the stone escarpment from the south, Wolf saw that their objective was already occupied by two Apaches worming their way up the sheer wall, while their tribesmen were engaged in the frontal attack. The Indians were so focused on the tricky footing, they did not notice the visitors some fifty yards behind them, and the rapid gunfire obliterated any other sounds.

"Volunteers to take those two out?" Wolf asked.

"I've got the one on the right," Jael said.

"I'll take left," Cal said.

They each pulled Winchesters from their scabbards, levered cartridges into the chambers, aimed, and squeezed triggers. The crack of Cal's rifle followed Jael's by no more than ten seconds. Two bodies toppled from the rock wall and landed on the earth at the feet of their staked horses.

"Let's move," Wolf yelled.

The riders split off, Wolf and Jael heading for the east end of the escarpment. When they reached the corner, Wolf checked to confirm that Cal and North Star were positioned. He raised his hand and the riders swept around the wall and into the open. Wolf was pleased to find the Apaches afoot, obviously trying to make more difficult targets as they inched their ways toward the trapped defenders. Now, though, they would be at a disadvantage against attackers on horseback. Wolf had found it easier to use his handgun from horseback and unholstered his Army Colt and swung it around, seeking a target among the shocked Apaches who were obviously confused and rattled at the appearance of the strangers.

A warrior who had been bellying his way toward the besieged leaped from the earth and aimed his rifle at Wolf just before Wolf squeezed the trigger and a slug tore into the Apache's jaw. Before he hit the ground, another struck him in the chest. The black stallion with the ghostly face wheeled at his rider's gentle nudge, and Wolf placed a shot in another warrior's shoulder before Jael drove a bullet into the wounded man's neck with her Winchester, untroubled by firing her long gun from a racing mount.

Wolf turned again to see Cal riding two retreating Apaches down, splitting one's head like a melon with his rifle butt. An instant later, he leaped from his horse with skinning knife in hand and landed on the other fleeing Indian, flattening the man face-down and then grasping his long hair, yanking the warrior's head back and slicing his throat, ignoring the spewing blood that spattered his own face.

It was all over in minutes. Wolf walked around the battleground to confirm there were no survivors. Thankfully, he found none and was spared the unpleasant task of finishing a kill. He took no pleasure from killing or maiming men, but he feared these would not be his last during the search for Tabby. It was kill or be killed, he reminded himself.

Chapter 18

JAEL, DELGADO, AND Sundog retrieved the horses and mules that had been secreted away pending the Apache showdown while the others disposed of the bodies, mostly by dropping them in gullies and pushing dirt and sand over the corpses. Jael knew scavengers would find the remains anyway and dig them out for dining, but she supposed it was the civilized thing to do. She guessed her years living as a Comanche had dulled her sensibilities about such things. She thought it unlikely the efforts would delay discovery by the Apaches' fellow tribesmen.

After the burials, canteens were filled from the spring-fed pool at the base of Mushroom Rock and then the horses led in to drink their fill. Jael sensed that Wolf was uneasy as his eyes scanned the horizon. She shared his discomfort. They occupied a natural fortress for the moment, but a large body of warriors could trap them here and eventually overrun their position.

"We need to talk," Wolf said, "but not here." He spoke to Delgado. "Is there someplace we can get to before sundown that gives us better cover than this place?"

"There is a small canyon not far from here. Water, trees, and some grass. But it is blind, only one way in and out."

"I would prefer high ground where we're looking down instead of up. A canyon, especially a blind one, could turn into a bear trap if the wrong folks find us there."

"Yes. I understand. We came across a place atop a wide scalped ridge in the foothills where we stayed a night. It is sheltered by mesquite and other brush and scrub pines, and it provides a view of the surrounding hills and some grazing for the horses on the west side of the ridge—nice shallow stream cuts through downslope on that side, so we'd have a water supply. It is about another half day's ride to the Apache stronghold from there."

"That sounds more like what I've got in mind."

"It will be a challenge to reach this place before sundown."

"Then we had better be riding."

Delgado and Sundog ranged ahead of the others, searching out landmarks that would lead the party back to their former campsite. Listening to the men speak to each other in their native tongue, Jael became intrigued with launching the task of learning yet another language. North Star, although raised among his father's Pueblo people, had been born to a Navajo mother. Dezba was also a schoolteacher in the schools established by missionaries near Taos and had taught her sons to speak fluent English and Navajo in addition to their father's Pueblo. Jael, who had been named She Who Speaks by her Comanche family in early recognition of her affinity for languages, had come to realize that for an inexplicable reason her mind processed languages almost as easily as some folks digested food. Her gift had leveraged her into a position as counselor to Quanah, unprecedented status for a woman among the Comanche. Now she was responsible for the law firm's growing niche practice representing the Comanche, Kiowa, and several smaller tribes. The Navajo, even the Apaches, seemed natural client prospects in the years ahead. Thus, as they rode, Jael began quizzing North Star about elementary words of the Diné language and various nuances of the tongue. She simply could not pass up this opportunity.

The party reached the destination a good half-hour before sundown, and Wolf seemed satisfied with the campsite. Their presence would not be an announcement of arrival to potential enemies, but a rider in the vicinity could spot them easily enough during daylight. They would be in the saddle before sunrise, Jael figured. Meanwhile, tonight would be a cold camp and a meal of jerky and dried biscuits. They could not hit the blankets soon enough as far as she was concerned.

After staking out the horses, the group gathered about Wolf and claimed spots on the ground to sit. Jael snatched up a bedroll blanket to wrap around her shoulders. Within hearing distance, North Star strolled the camp's perimeter, keeping a watch out for unwelcome visitors.

Wolf said, "We haven't had much time to talk. Delgado, you and Sundog have been out here for days. You're convinced the captives are a half day's ride from this place?"

Delgado turned to Sundog and spoke at some length in Navajo. The young man responded, shaking his head in agreement, it appeared. Jael recognized a few words she had heard from North Star's brief lessons, but she was more interested in the cadence of the language during the conversation. Few understood the importance of rhythm in speaking a foreign tongue. Language was more than mere recitation of words.

When the two Diné finished their discussion, Delgado said. "There are two Mimbres villages a day's ride apart. The larger one was being set up during our scout, and we had to hide sometimes, because Apaches were going there in small groups, including some families. They seemed disorganized and fearful they were being followed."

Wolf said, "I'm guessing that was Victorio's band. They broke away from the reservation while you were scouting out this way. They were likely worried about the Army being on their tails, but from what we were told, the military wants more troops assigned to Fort Apache and Camp Huachuca before they take to the field. Fort Defiance is designated as the Navaho Indian Agency headquarters and maintains only enough troops to service and police the reservation. We can't wait for the Army, and, frankly, I don't think we want them around if we are going to get the captives out alive."

Delgado said, "That explains the new encampment. The prisoners should be in the smaller village, and that would be El Gato's band."

"Tell me about the setting again," Wolf asked.

"A half day's ride to the north base of the mountain where the village is located. From the north, the village can be entered only by a single file trail up the mountainside. It is guarded, and it would be impossible to attack from that side."

Wolf said, "Well, we aren't going to attack the village. But even if the Army couldn't reach them from the north, they could lay siege to the trail, so there has got to be a back door."

Delgado said, "Southeast. It is still a steep climb, but there is a wide trail that follows a stream that cuts through a narrow canyon that opens into a valley below. A narrow trail follows the stream on the other side. There is much grass there and the ruins of a house and buildings that were part of a great Spanish hacienda before the Apaches drove The People away many years ago. These mountains have been strongholds for many Apache bands."

"And the stronghold is on the Mexican side of the border, I assume?"

"Yes, this makes it more difficult for American soldiers to attack, although the officers have been known to claim ignorance of the border's location from time to time. There is no line drawn in the earth. We are not in Mexico here, but I can only guess when we pass that invisible crossing. Further east, there is the Rio Grande to mark the divide, of course."

Wolf said, "We're not bound by any rules. We'll go where we need to go. How long would it take us to get into the village from the canyon side?"

"From here and on foot, I would guess a long day, maybe more, allowing for rest and a few naps, to the canyon's mouth. Less than a half day from there to the village," Delgado said. "I cannot be certain because there seem to be many twists in the canyon's route. We did not go beyond the mouth. The distance is not so far from here, but the best trails pass between mountains and are very rough and steep. We had to lead our horses, but I would not do that again. They would be a hindrance if a man needed to move fast. A horse's legs would be in danger on these slopes. And there will be guards posted along the canyon walls, as well."

Wolf observed, "Horses might be better left someplace. What bothers me most is that escape would be slow, too, and we would be deeper into Mexico and the mountains. And we still have the question of how we remove the prisoners from the village."

Jael had noticed Cal's sober silence during the conversation and was surprised when he finally spoke. "For what it's worth, I think we ought to have a few guns at both entrances. We might need to get them out both ways, and somebody needs to be there to help them. Either way, it seems it wouldn't hurt to have a ruckus created at both places. Mix them up a bit."

"You're making sense, Cal," Wolf said. "But there are so few of us, I hate to split up. Maybe we don't have a choice."

Delgado said, "If we remove the hostages from the village, El Gato will chase us deep into Diné lands. We can race for Fort Defiance, but with women and children and some riding double, we will never get far enough ahead of them. Defiance is many days from here."

"We do have the spare mounts and mules. Some of the children are small enough to ride double without slowing us," Wolf commented.

Jael chided herself for being selfish. She had only been thinking of Tabby, her best friend. But there were others who could not be left behind. This was becoming increasingly complicated, and she despaired for a few moments at the seemingly hopeless task facing them. Until this moment it had not crossed her mind that she might never see Josh, Michael and Rylee again. Then, she reminded herself, not for the first time, that she could well have died with her parents during the Comanche raid on their wagon all those years ago. She had enjoyed a life since that she might never have had.

Wolf said, "We need to sleep on this, but I have a thought. Manuelito planned to ride out with another search party. They may have even left the village by now. But they have no idea where the Apache stronghold is. It seems to me that direction-wise, they have no place to head but south."

"That is true," Delgado said.

"We can't wait for him, and they wouldn't do us any good till the captives are out of the village, but I would like to send Sundog to intercept them and lead the party this way. If we get away, we'll take the same route we took from Defiance to here. Hopefully, we can run into Manuelito's party before Apaches overtake us."

Delgado translated to Sundog, and the young Navajo replied.

"He can do this," Delgado said.

Chapter 19

TABITHA WAS DISAPPOINTED when a warrior rode into the village early morning and announced the hunting party would be returning by nightfall. Women were instructed to be ready to skin and cut the beeves that had been killed and packed on crude racks for dragging to the camp. The party had also captured two prisoners for torture, the warrior had added gleefully. The hunters had returned three or four days early, and now El Gato's conjugal visits would doubtless resume. To add to her misery, Cactus Bloom's jealousy would heat up, and Tabitha could count on more violent beatings.

She had taken advantage of El Gato's absence to scout out the landscape that surrounded the village. She had learned that there was greater expanse to the mesa than her initial guess. The flat dropped off some at the south end onto a lower level consisting of lush grasses that overlooked a narrow canyon where the stream tumbled over its rocky bed on a twisting journey to an outlet that was hidden from her view at the canyon's edge. Each time she had investigated, she caught sight of a sentry on a ledge protruding from the canyon wall, and there were doubtless others lurking along the path of the stream's descent. She had wondered more than once if the water would be deep enough to allow her to simply leap in and ride the rush to the canyon floor. It was a few feet deep at the mesa level, flowing gently on the flat, but as it poured over the edge and rushed down the canyon, she would risk hammering by the stony bed.

She thought she would have a chance at such an escape alone, but she had already decided she would not leave without the other Navajo captives. That drastically reduced her options, if not eliminating them entirely. She could just stay and endure whatever came her way. If she obeyed, El Gato would not likely kill her. When he learned she was carrying his child, which she now concluded was probable, her life would be further secured. Her treatment by Cactus Bloom would likely not improve, however.

Eventually, the Apaches would return to the reservation, and she could contact the Army for her release. She could wait a year if it came to that. But three years? Five? And El Gato could be killed in the meantime. He was both captor and protector. She had always blazed her own trail through life, made her own decisions whether good or bad. It was alien to her nature to be a mere puppet dancing to some man's whimsy. No, she would find a way out of this place soon. She would present it to the abducted Navajos, and they could join her or not as they chose.

Early afternoon, Walks Far appeared at Tabitha's wickiup with her baby, Peace Searcher, propped on her hip. Tabitha sat in front of the wickiup next to a small stack of coyote skins, which she had been assigned by the senior wife to cut and stitch together to make a blanket or winter cloak. She looked up when she sensed her friend had been watching her.

"I am sorry," Tabitha said, "I did not hear you—I never hear you. I was trying to plan my work so Cactus Bloom will not complain, and you move so quietly."

Walks Far dropped to the ground near Tabitha and planted the baby in her lap. "No matter how Ta-Bee fix, she not like. Do good, maybe no beat Ta-Bee."

Tabitha began stitching with thick sinew tied to a thick porcupine quill. She knew Cactus Bloom possessed steel needles acquired from traders, but the woman was not about to relinquish one to her husband's other woman. "Her beatings are not so often or as violent now. I think they are mostly to show me that she can. She may sense that I am very near to fighting back. I have reason not to permit her treatment now."

"The baby?"

Tabitha froze mid-stitch and stared at her friend. "You know?"

Walks Far giggled. "I guess. Now know."

"You will not say anything to anyone?"

"No tell." She rubbed her abdomen. "But this tell some time."

She let loose the fear that had been crippling her. "I do not want El Gato's child. I do not know what I should do."

"Ta-Bee's child, too. El Gato stallion. Womans like him. Make good babies." She hesitated. "Crow Woman can make baby go away."

"You mean abort it?"

"Not know 'abort.' She kills. Take powders. Be sick, but baby gone."

She did not want to hear this. She had decided instantly when Walks Far said, "Ta-Bee's child, too." El Gato may have planted the seed, but she was the one that would nurture and grow it, and she would never let the son-of-a-bitch lay claim to her baby. She would not let her child be born in this place, where El Gato would direct his or her future and the mother would have no say.

"I must leave."

Walks Far's face revealed her sadness. "Know this. I say will help."

"You still would? I know you said you would not tell Moon Watcher, but can you really keep this from him?"

"No tell."

"I do not want to cause trouble between you."

"I am Diné. You say what Ta-Bee want. Talk to Sunrise."

"I will think on this, but I want to leave within ten days. You will not come with us?"

"Must stay with Moon Watcher. Good father. Kind husband." She lifted her hand, pressing two fingers together. "Moon Watcher and Walks Far like this."

A wave mixed with sadness and envy swept over her. She and Oliver Wolf had been like that, and like a fool she had broken the link and now was carrying another man's child. She could never face him again. If she escaped El Gato, perhaps Still Water, if she was alive, would help her carve out a home with the Diné.

Later, the hunting party arrived with the bounty of rustled beef and two wild-eyed, obviously terror-stricken, prisoners, who were attired like Mexican vaqueros, probably night riders for the herd from which the cattle were stolen. Tabitha was heartsick for the men. They had no value to the band for trade or integration into the tribe. They had been brought to the village for the occupants' entertainment by way of abuse and torture. She had secretly watched such proceedings in the Comanche village on one occasion and turned away when she could endure no more. And she had heard that Comanche were amateurs compared to the Apaches when it came to inflicting pain and suffering upon their prisoners.

Walks Far sprung to her feet and scurried away to help with skinning and butchering of the stolen cattle. Her parting words were, "Will talk, Ta-Bee. Two suns."

Tabitha picked up her stitching materials and coyote skins and placed them in the wickiup. She knew that Cactus Bloom would expect her to appear to participate in the methodical process that included the skinning of the animals, cutting the meat from the bones and hanging strips on racks to dry. Some of the meat would be roasted this evening during a big feast, followed by the hollow, steady beat of drums and frenzied dancing to celebrate the hunters' return and success. She suspected the night would culminate with torture of the hapless prisoners.

Cactus Bloom was waiting with her usual disapproving frown and scolding eyes when Tabby arrived at the wickiup of El Gato's senior wife. She handed Tabitha a keen-bladed skinning knife and pointed to one of the dead steers that Walks Far had already started gutting. Tabitha was glad to join her friend in the work. As she walked toward Walks Far with the knife in her hand, her fingers caressed the ornately carved hilt. The work of a Mexican craftsman no doubt, a narrow blade suitable for skinning but easily adapted to a fine killing instrument. If only she could take this knife and secret it away someplace. She felt so naked and vulnerable without a weapon.

It occurred to her that she could "misplace" the knife and hide it somewhere to retrieve later. Cactus Bloom would beat her for losing it, but the woman's contempt for her husband's second wife might cause her to see Tabitha as stupid enough to lose it. If she said something to El Gato though, he would see through the ruse in a second.

Another woman was helping process the cattle carcasses where Walks Far was working, so they were unable to do more than exchange signs. Little Grasshopper spoke no English, and Tabitha, as a foreigner, felt it would have been rude to impose her tongue in the presence of one who did not understand it. Thus, she maintained her silence for the most part while the Mimbres women chattered, interrupting only with occasional questions for Walks Far about disposition of the meat. By dusk the women were distributing meat among the villagers, and choice pieces, including livers and tongue were roasting on cooking fires.

Tabitha, claiming an urgency to pee, told Walks Far she would deliver portions of the meat to Cactus Bloom on her way to the common waste grounds. Walks Far assured her they were nearly finished and there was no need to return. When she departed, she veered past her own wickiup and tossed the knife inside. Then she went to the wickiup Cactus Bloom shared with El Gato. Thankfully, neither was there, so she quickly hung the strips for drying on the empty rack and dropped the other meat chunks in the kettle near the door. She went to the common waste grounds and relieved herself, glad that several other women were also squatting nearby and could verify her stop if asked. Then she hurried back to her wickiup and snatched up the pilfered knife, lifting her Mexican skirt and securing the weapon to her thigh with a rawhide strip.

She rushed to the steam to wash away the blood and fluids that had clung to her arms and legs during the cattle butchering. When she arrived, she saw two women, who seemed not to notice her, bathing upstream. She slipped off her moccasins and waded to the other side to the rotting stump of a pine tree that she had identified as a potential hiding place some days earlier. Casting her eyes about to be certain she was not being observed, Tabitha removed the knife and pushed it deep into the soft decayed center, out of sight and easy to remove when the time was right. She disrobed and splashed into the frigid water, making noise now to attract attention. The women upstream looked her way, and she waved but got no response. Perhaps, that was not how Apache women acknowledged another. She had not noticed but did not care. They saw her. That was all that mattered.

That night she lay in her wickiup, not knowing if the missing knife had been noticed, wondering if El Gato would visit, and promising she would be attentive, if he did. After all, she had essentially become a whore, she thought, buying her life with her carnal services. Was it that much different from what the ladies of the bordello did? She hoped that this first night back in the village Cactus Bloom would demand his attention. Although the woman had not thwarted the taking of a second wife, Cactus Bloom had not relinquished her hold on El Gato entirely, and he seemed wary of her temper.

The drums and chanting were echoing across the mountain tops now. Thank God, her presence had not been commanded. She supposed it was something of an optional social event. The sounds made her shudder and they went on and on. She finally dropped off to sleep to be awakened suddenly less than an hour later by the incessant screaming of the captured vaqueros. Another reason El Gato would not visit this night, she thought. He would not have missed a moment of the horror that was being visited upon those poor men. And it gave her another reason to despise the father of the child growing in her womb.

Chapter 20

DELGADO SIGNALED A pause several miles before the rescue party reached the area he and Sundog had identified as an entry to the trail that led to the Mimbres Apaches' mountain lair. "Ahead is a break in the trees off this trail. When you turn into the trees and continue south for a short distance, you reach the north trail to the village. Eyes will be watching you from the rocks above. You cannot surprise them, although since they are so many, and we are so few, surprise would be no advantage."

Wolf said, "I never expected to attempt an attack. We need to find a way to separate the captives from the main body and then make a run for it."

Cal said, "Wolf, you ain't making sense. We don't know who they're holding there or how many."

"I am going to ride into the village and find out."

Cal gave him and incredulous look. "I don't think I heard you right."

"That's why I brought the pack mule with all the trade goods. I'm going to be a trader. Maybe trade for some of the captives—at least for those they were going to sell anyway, if they're still held in the village. I'll offer gold for the whole lot if they're open to it."

"That's crazy. They'll just kill you and help themselves."

"The tribes don't like to cut off their trading contacts. The Apaches have got even more incentive since the Army is going to take to the field against them soon. And I won't carry the gold with me the first trip. If we make a deal, I'll come back for it. Most Indians have a sense of honor. Their word will stick unless you give them what they see as cause to go back on it."

"So you think it will be as easy as ransom?" Cal asked.

"I am saying I don't know, but we should give it a try. Do you think you and Delgado can make it to the south entrance without losing your scalps?"

"Damn right we can, but what do you want us to do there?" Cal asked.

"I'm going to take the pack mule with me up the north trail. North Star and Jael will wait here with the gold I brought. You can kick in what you want."

"All of it," Cal snapped. "But you haven't said why Delgado and I are headed south."

"If Tabby or any or the captives make an escape that way, somebody's got to be there to help them find their way out. Otherwise, they've got no idea where to go and likely nothing to defend themselves with. From what Delgado said, it will take you two days to get set up in the canyon. Hold out there for double that. If nothing happens, head back this way and find whoever's left of us. . . and get the hell out."

"I don't like it. We won't know what the hell's going on up at this end."

"We can't write a script for this, but if we are going to get any of the captives out, we have to be prepared at both of the exits from the village."

"I just want to see that Little Sis gets out of that place. And I would sure like to kill the bastard that took her."

"Do you think I don't want to free Tabby? Do you have a better plan?"

Cal gave a deep sigh. "Guess not. I'll unpack my gold. You're going in then and will come back to get the gold if you strike a deal?"

"That's the plan I'm starting with."

Delgado said, "We can go faster and safer without the horses. It would be hard to keep the horses from being seen, so I am still in favor of leaving them behind. I think North Star and Jael should head back to where we stayed last night with the extra horses and mule. There is tree shelter and water and grass for the horses and mules."

Wolf said, "Good idea. It's just a few hours back and puts a bit more distance between the village and our spare mounts, as well as the gold. Apaches can show up anytime, but it's a fair bet most of the activity goes through the south entrance deeper into Mexico away from the U. S. Army."

Jael said, "You take the lead with the pack mule. I'll follow."

Wolf bristled. Jael could be as stubborn as Tabby, and he had wondered when they were going to have a showdown. "This is a one-man job."

"One man, maybe, but add one woman to the venture."

"It doesn't serve any purpose for two of us to ride in there."

"How much Apache do you speak?"

The language card was a good one, and she had played that one from the beginning. He knew he could not play a better one. "Sign language. The leaders will know sign language. North Star said El Gato spoke some English." He turned to North Star. "Didn't you?"

"Well, I didn't hear much, since he knocked me out, but Tabby said he spoke just a little."

Jael said, "Even if someone speaks English, they aren't going to be talking English to each other, and you won't have any idea what they're saying. And I understand the language better than I speak it. Like I said, you can take the lead with the pack mule, and I will follow—whether you agree or not."

He had already lost this one. There was no reason to aggravate her further. Wolf looked skyward. It was nearing high noon. "We'll ride back to the watering hole where North Star will stay with the extra horses. Delgado and Cal can put together what they need for their trek through the mountains. They can get a start this afternoon. The trading expedition will hold off till morning."

Chapter 21

ON HER WAY to collect water from the stream the morning after the Apaches' celebration, Tabitha passed the ceremonial circle that was located just outside the village and caught a glimpse of the two naked bodies staked out near the stone fire altar. Buzzards circled in the bright morning sky, drifting lower with each turn and casting dark specter-like shadows over the earth below. Tabitha prayed that the men were dead now and their misery ended. She tried to fight off the urge to move on and remove the grisly scene from her sight, but she could not walk on without knowing.

She approached the site of the torture, stopping when she was near enough to confirm the condition of the men. She flinched and felt just a moment of weakness before turning away. Thank God they were dead. Their genitals had been amputated, of course, to assure they would not reproduce in some afterlife—the Comanche did such things and she understood it to be a practice of many tribes. One man's eyes had been burned to dark holes, the other disemboweled. Countless slashes on the bodies and missing fingers and toes attested to the work that had taken place here. The vultures were inching closer, almost disregarding her presence in their enthusiasm to get about the business of cleaning up the scene. By nightfall there would be only bones remaining to be tidied up and carried off by dogs or wild creatures sneaking in at dusk.

Tabitha moved on and completed her task at the stream. When she took the earthenware water jugs to Cactus Bloom's wickiup, she found El Gato and his senior wife standing in front, obviously engaged in a heated argument. When Cactus Bloom saw Tabitha, she wheeled and pointed at her, screaming something unintelligible but decidedly uncomplimentary. Tabitha set the jugs down and started to make a discreet retreat when El Gato grabbed her wrist and harshly yanked her back.

His angry eyes were within a foot of her own when he spoke, "Knife. Cactus Bloom say take knife."

Tabitha had been prepared for this question. "What knife? I do not know what you are talking about? I did not take any knife."

"Knife. When cow come." He turned to Cactus Bloom, who had a smug smile on her face now that the blame had shifted. He said something to her in Apache, Tabitha understanding only the word for Walks Far.

Cactus Bloom rushed away while El Gato turned his attention back to Tabitha. "Ta-Bee knife. No die."

She took his words as a statement that he would kill her if she did not surrender the knife. "I do not have your knife. I cannot give you what I do not have." She was determined to stick with her story at the risk of her life, realizing he might not even understand what she was saying.

El Gato clutched the neck of her blouse and tore it off, tossing her to the ground with the force of his sinewy arm. While she was down, he bent over and latched on to her skirt, pulling it off as he dragged her on the rocky earth in front of the wickiup, leaving her lying naked in the dust while he slipped into the wickiup.

Tabitha struggled to her knees, preparing to spring up and run, when he emerged with the three-tongued whip in hand. The two children peered out the opening wide-eyed and tight-lipped. She had felt the whip's bite before, but Cactus Bloom was inept with the instrument and not nearly so strong. Her lashes stung but did not cut. She had felt the slices of a whip before and knew first-hand what damage it could do when wielded by a skilled administrator. The whip's lashes were longer than the white man's riding quirt but far shorter than a bullwhip. She figured it mattered little if snapped by a man liked El Gato.

She stood and faced him to plead her case again. "I do not have the knife. Please. I do not have it."

"Lie."

Before she could turn away, the whip arched forward, and the tongues sliced down her chest, leaving three bloody lines like a cat's claw marks on the breast he had already maimed. She turned away as the whip cracked again, catching her on the hip this time but cutting deeper. She went to the ground again, curling with back and buttocks upward, her instinctive reaction to protect her child. She braced for the next attack, but then she heard a woman screaming, a familiar voice—Walks Far.

Tabitha turned her head and saw her friend facing El Gato, yelling at him fearlessly. Of course, the band's chief did not dare attack Moon Watcher's wife. Tabitha had learned that El Gato's hold on the band was tenuous and that Moon Watcher's diplomatic skills were the leader's links to those who might otherwise challenge or rebel.

Tabitha started to climb to her feet as Walks Far gathered up her friend's blouse and skirt and came to her.

Others with curious eyes had gathered at a discreet distance and were watching now, although no one seemed especially excited. Tabitha had seen other such male and female fusses during her capture, although none so dramatic as a public disrobing and whipping. She was long past any embarrassment over her nakedness, but she gladly slipped back into her tattered garments, feeling somehow a bit less vulnerable.

As she dressed, El Gato stood and watched, face grim and arms folded with the whip handle still grasped in one hand. He spoke to Walks Far and she turned to Tabitha, "I talk for him and you. English hard for him."

"An interpreter. That would be a good thing. He says I have a knife."

"Does Ta-Bee have knife?"

It pained her to lie to her friend. She tried to word her response to avoid a falsehood directed to Walks Far. "Tell him I say I do not have the knife. Ask him why he thinks I would have one."

Walks Far's eyes told Tabitha that her friend had already concluded she had the knife. Dutifully, she conveyed the message to El Gato, and they engaged in an extended dialogue before Walks Far spoke to Tabitha again. "He say Cactus Bloom give knife to skin and cut cows. Ta-Bee no give back. El Gato say Ta-Bee want kill him with knife. Say he kill Ta-Bee, so she no kill him."

"Tell him Cactus Bloom was not here when I brought the meat. I hung the strips on racks and left the other meat in a pot with the knife. She must have lost it or someone else took it." Tabby explained how she had gone to the waste field and bathed in the stream after that and others had seen her there. "He can ask the others if they saw me with a knife. He has already seen that I do not carry it on my body. He can search my wickiup now—before I would have a chance to hide it."

"He no fool. Others mean nothing. Ta-Bee not show knife if have. I want help but story no good."

"Tell him what I said. Then tell him I carry his child. If El Gato kills me, he kills his son. If he beats me, he may harm his son or cause me to lose his boy. Say I promise I would never harm my son's father."

Tabitha watched and listened while the two chattered back and forth. At first the tones were angry but later softened some. A glance at the glum Cactus Bloom told her that the senior wife was not happy with the direction the conversation was taking—unhappiness with the prospect of the forthcoming child. Walks Far had told her that Cactus Bloom appeared unlikely to bear more children given the lapse of time since the younger child was born.

There was a pause in the conversation, and Walks Far turned back to Tabitha. "Ta-Bee say boy. How know this?"

She had indicated a male child because she had guessed the premium a war chief would place on a fledgling warrior. "Tell him that white women know the moment the seed is planted. It is a message from our spirit."

"See why Ta-Bee write words. Good liar." She told El Gato what Tabitha had said. He looked dubious but nodded.

The crisis had seemingly cooled for the moment. Walks Far joined El Gato and Tabitha on the walk to Tabitha's wickiup and remained until El Gato had overturned all the blankets and searched the sparse contents. When he was finished, he said nothing and walked away.

Walks Far said, "Come back. Bring medicines for hurts. Talk. Have talk."

As Walks Far hurried away, Tabitha worried about the ominous tone of her friend's voice. She apparently did not think all was settled. Of course not. It would not be until she escaped this place. But at least there was a reprieve. She lived and so did her unborn child. She retrieved the furs that El Gato had tossed about her wickiup during his futile search for the knife, deciding continuation of her work on the blanket would be a distraction while she rethought her latest predicament.

An hour later, Walks Far returned with some salves and cleaned and treated the whip lash wounds. Her friend commented that the soft flesh of the breast might bear scars but the hip not so much. The pain relief was instant and Walks Far promised to return to apply additional treatments until the lacerations were healed.

They sat silently together in the wickiup, Tabitha waiting for Walks Far to speak. Finally, the Navajo-Apache woman spoke. "El Gato fears Ta-Bee. Why?"

"Fears me? I think not. You saw what he was doing to me. I am no physical threat to him."

"Even with the knife Ta-Bee hide?"

So the truth was on the table. "I would kill him only to defend my life and my child's. I prefer to leave without violence. I do not know how that is possible."

"I see death Ta-Bee stay. El Gato. Ta-Bee. Maybe both. I help. Tell me how. Soon."

EL GATO CAME to the wickiup that night, apparently unconcerned about the pain he had inflicted upon her that morning. His fingers brushed the ground that fringed the robe and blankets, evidently confirming that the disputed knife was not secreted there. She was naked under the blankets, unsurprised at his visit. When he slipped in beside her, she was more than compliant this time, caressing him, teasing him, feigning enthusiasm. He seemed wary and nervous at her touch at first, confused by her aggression.

Her attention seemed to spur him to his mission, and he finished quickly and pulled away preparing to slip away until she grasped his hip and encouraged him to stay. It did not take her long to incite his interest, for she had shared the bed of an innovative and skillful lover and been an apt and enthusiastic pupil. He surrendered quickly to her manipulation with pleasurable sighs and grunts. When it was over, she hated herself almost as much as she despised El Gato.

He fell asleep and stayed most of the night for the first time. Strangely, Tabitha slept soundly beside him. When she awakened, he was gone, but she was left with a sense that something significant had happened during their coupling. She had discovered a weapon she might exploit that could be as useful to her as the hidden knife, perhaps more so.

Chapter 22

El Gato returned to the wickiup he shared with Cactus Bloom well before sunrise and crawled into his own robe, not wanting to wake his wife and deal with the tantrum that would doubtless be triggered by his long absence. Sleep eluded him as he thought about his interlude with Ta-Bee just hours earlier, and he sensed his member stiffening again. She was, indeed, a warrior woman. For a brief time, she had taken charge, and he had not encountered this in his experience with a woman.

Only Moon Watcher suspected the reason for his obsession with the woman he first saw near a mountain stream. He wanted a Lozen, a female warrior, to ride with him into battle, to share his robe not as a servant but as an equal during the night. And now his Lozen would bear his son. The son would be the greatest Apache warrior ever. He truly believed this. But now he must bring this woman to his side. He would never let her go, but he was far from trusting her. They were at war, and he must negotiate a peace and make an alliance with her.

Lozen was Victorio's sister, a legendary warrior who rode with her brother into battle. She had the status of a sub-chief who often led her own war party. She was beautiful and a muscular physical presence. El Gato had pursued her affections some years earlier, hoped for a marriage to the warrior woman and, incidentally, to become a part of the great war chief's family. But Lozen had spurned him as she had many others, and he could only worship her from afar.

After the pain of Lozen's rejection had dulled, he decided that his quest would be to find the warrior woman he felt he was destined to have at his side. In the meantime, he had married Cactus Bloom to satisfy his carnal needs and to perpetuate his bloodline. She was a handsome woman, temperamental but ultimately obedient. She had no interest in the warrior skills, and he had not expected it. Then, he had seen Ta-Bee that day. She was his Lozen.

Ta-Bee would have the courage and the skills to fight at his side and draw Victorio's envy, but these same attributes could also be launched against him. That was his dilemma. He realized now his strategy had been flawed.

He had tried to beat her into submission. The warrior in her would never submit to physical force. Such tactics only spurred her to fight back. No, he must hold back his anger and impatience and forge the alliance with some indulgence and respect. She had seemingly opened her spirit to such a possibility just hours earlier. He must try. If it did not work, he could kill her after his son's birth.

EARLY THAT AFTERNOON, El Gato showed up when Tabitha was sitting in front of her wickiup, grinding corn with a stone on a large concave rock that served as a natural bowl. She looked up at him questioningly. She ordinarily saw little of him during the day, and she hoped that he was not going to reignite the dispute over the knife.

He was silent for a time, his eyes roaming over her body as if making an appraisal for some purpose. Finally, he spoke. "Shoot gun?" He positioned his arms to mimic firing a rifle.

"You are asking me if I can shoot a rifle? Yes."

He seemed dubious, but said, "Go now," pointing to an open area west of the village backed by a rock wall where the mountain climbed beyond the mesa.

She shrugged and obeyed, remembering the admonition of Moon Watcher and Walks Far that obedience was her key to life here. She could not imagine what the war chief had in mind, but his mood seemed more troubled than violent. Tabitha got up and strolled through the village toward the flat beyond.

She waited alone, casting her eyes about for information to put to memory that would aid in her escape. She had decided she would wait no more than a week and, if the opportunity did not present itself, she would make her own. Looking back toward the village, she saw three men and a woman coming her way. One was El Gato. She recognized his walk by now. Moon Watcher was with the party, and as they drew nearer, she saw Walks Far behind him. She did not know the other warrior.

El Gato clutched a rifle in each hand. The others carried armloads of something. When they approached, Tabitha recognized the objects as tus, wicker jugs of various sizes, twined from willow, sumac and mulberry sprigs and sealed with pine gum. They could be used to store water or virtually any substance like whites did with glass or pottery jugs. The Apache women were quite proficient at the art, and Tabitha had been trying with some difficulty to acquire the skill. Cactus Bloom had given up on her, but the ever-optimistic Walks Far had remained hopeful.

She also saw that El Gato carried her precious Henry. Whore that Tabitha felt she had become, she wondered what she could do for him that would get it back in her hands.

"What are we going to do?" she asked.

Walks Far intervened and spoke in Apache to El Gato. He responded at length before Walks Far turned back to Tabitha. "El Gato and Ta-Bee have contest. See who shoot more tus. You use rifle. Give back. No try shoot El Gato, or Wolf Eyes kill."

Tabitha looked at the stocky Apache who now had his own rifle raised waist-high and pointed at her. "What happens if I win?"

Walks Far repeated her question, and the warriors all laughed. Then El Gato replied. Walks Far translated. "Keep rifle."

Tabitha resisted showing her elation. This offer removed any possibility she would spare El Gato's ego during the match. She could not fathom any purpose for this silly test, but she was caught up in the game now.

There was more discussion among the Apaches, and then Walks Far and Moon Watcher carried half of the jugs out into the flat and lined up two groups of five each before returning. Tabitha judged that the jugs were just short of twenty-five yards out. The mountain wall made a decent backdrop, and the sun was not a factor yet. She eyed the guns still clasped in El Gato's hands. Besides her

Henry, he held an old Sharps, a bit heavy for horseback fighting, she thought, but the Sharps' five hundred-yard distance accuracy with a good marksman far exceeded the Henry. In her experience among the Comanche, however, she had found their proficiency with a long gun mediocre at best. She hoped El Gato was no better.

El Gato handed Tabitha the Henry and five .44 rimfire cartridges, a third of what the rifle would hold in its magazine. "Shoot," he pointed to the group of tus on her left.

She pushed the cartridges into the magazine and levered one into the chamber. She placed the rifle butt to her shoulder, sighted and squeezed the trigger. The rifle cracked and one of the jugs split and toppled. Four more quick shots took down the others.

El Gato stared at her, his eyes showing new respect. He turned to his own weapon, firing more slowly but repeating her feat. He grunted in satisfaction and gave instructions to Moon Watcher and Walks Far. They took the remaining jugs out on the flat and doubled the distance this time when they lined up the targets.

This time, El Gato fired first, taking down four of the five jugs and nodding with satisfaction when he stepped back. Tabitha figured her opponent had the advantage here with his more powerful firearm, but the jugs were within the Henry's range. She did not fire so quickly this time, aiming carefully and squeezing the trigger deliberately with each shot. She downed all five jugs. Without a word, El Gato wheeled and walked back to the village, followed by Moon Watcher and Wolf Eyes. Tabitha watched them disappear into the village, caressing her faithful Henry with her fingertips and wondering what atrocity she might have visited upon herself.

"El Gato no like lose," Walks Far said solemnly.

"Is he angry? Will he beat me?"

"I think no. Moon Watcher say he want Ta-Bee be warrior woman."

"Warrior woman?"

"Like Lozen, Victorio sister. Fight enemies. Shoot rifle. Use spear and bow. Want Ta-Bee at side and be Apache. Share robe all times. Be great warrior."

"This is very strange. I do not understand."

"El Gato not hurt if be with him."

"You mean stay here? Stay with him always?"

"Yes."

"I cannot do that. I will not."

El Gato did not visit that night, thankfully. And when he entered the wickiup the next night, she could tell he was freshly bathed. He treated her respectfully, and he even praised her in his halting awkward English for her prowess with the rifle. He called her "warrior woman" and touched her cheek almost reverently. It occurred to her then that he was courting her in a way, seeking a loyalty and trust she could never give. She almost felt guilty at her use of this man who suddenly had displayed a few endearing qualities. He did not waste much time before he moved to her for the inevitable coupling. Not for the first time her mind transformed El Gato to Oliver Wolf when she responded to his touch and took special effort to give him pleasure. Again, when he was sated, El Gato lay beside her throughout the night.

Chapter 23

WOLF AND JAEL approached the trail that climbed the mountainside and led to the Apache stronghold on the mesa. They reined in and dismounted in the shelter of an aspen grove near the trail's entrance and studied the sheer stone walls they would be ascending.

Jael knew they had already been spotted. "They have already seen us, you know."

"Yep. You missed any chance to head back."

"Do you really believe I would have changed my mind?"

"No."

"Once we start up that trail, I'll raise my hand to show we come in peace. If a sentry shows himself, I will tell him we are traders. You should repeat in Apache. We'll play it by ear from there."

"I don't think gaining entry to the village will be a problem. Getting out could be."

Wolf nudged Owl onto the trail, leading the pack mule behind him. Jael followed, casting her eyes about as they rode at a snail's pace up the steep incline. No more than a quarter of the way up, she looked over her shoulder. Two Apache warriors entered the trail behind them, making no effort to close the gap but blocking the exit should they find a place on the trail wide enough to allow them to turn around. "Company behind us," she warned Wolf.

"Not surprised."

Wolf and Jael inched the horses around a curve on a narrow strip of trail, and Jael's stomach performed a few flips when she looked out over the edge of the precipice and caught a glimpse of what appeared to be a bottomless canyon. Eyes on the trail she reminded herself, only on the trail. Not long after they had negotiated the treacherous turn, they encountered a grim-faced warrior standing on a stone outcropping, looking down upon them, cradling a rifle poised to fire.

Wolf raised his hand. "We come in peace. We wish to trade with our friends."

Jael repeated his words in Apache.

The Apache seemed to ponder for a bit and then yelled to someone further up the slope. He signaled with his rifle barrel that they should go on.

"If you hadn't guessed," Jael said, "the warrior said they were to let us pass. He must have some authority."

"Let's hope."

They passed two additional sentries who offered stone faces and silence as they made their ways to the summit and rode out onto the mesa and saw the village not far away. A single warrior rode toward them from the village. They reined in and waited. When he came up, Jael was satisfied that his expression revealed neither hostility nor welcome. That would suffice for now. He was a handsome man, she thought, probably in his early thirties. He wore calf-high moccasins, breechclout, and a blue Mexican shirt with matching blue headband. There was no adornment to signify rank, but his bearing and dark, intelligent eyes suggested he was someone of importance.

He asked if they spoke Apache.

Jael replied in Apache, "I speak your language but not fluently. I am She Who Speaks, formerly of Quanah's Kwahadi Comanche band. This is White Wolf. We have goods to trade and other business we might do if The People are willing."

Responding in his own tongue, the warrior said, "I am Moon Watcher. It is possible we would trade. Do you bring guns?"

"We do not. We bring many goods of use to The People. Blankets, clothing, pots, pans, much foodstuffs."

Moon Watcher said, "Follow." He wheeled his horse and rode it at a walk toward the village.

Jael translated the conversation to Wolf as they rode. "I didn't mention the gold and said nothing about ransom. I think this warrior has influence but is cautious with his commitments."

As they moved toward the village, more mounted warriors fell in beside them, and Jael noticed the village coming to life with women and children rushing about and gathering to watch the new arrivals. She found herself a bit unnerved as the Apache outriders edged nearer, less confident that their visit would be welcomed. Wolf, though, appeared unfazed, sitting loose and relaxed in his saddle, eyes sweeping over the onlookers as he and Jael reached the edge of the village. The Apache who had given his name as Moon Watcher halted his horse. Jael and Wolf reined in behind him, as did the escorting warriors who studied the visitors with hostile and suspicious glares.

Wolf spoke, his face emotionless. "To your right near the scraggly pine. Don't even nod your head in recognition."

She turned her head and saw the tree before her eyes fastened on Tabitha's. Her friend gave a barely perceptible nod but returned no other sign of recognition. Jael averted her gaze to avoid attracting the attention of any observer. Moon Watcher dismounted and told Jael that she and Wolf should also dismount and wait until he returned. He explained to Jael that he must speak with El Gato to obtain approval for any trading that might be allowed. He also commented that the band had very little to offer in trade. As he departed, Jael cast a glance in the direction of the pine tree. Tabitha had disappeared.

The villagers and the warrior escort backed off some during the wait for Moon Watcher's return. The initial excitement had evidently burned out because some seemed to lose interest in the visitors and drift away. Standing between their horses, Wolf and Jael took inventory of their situation.

Jael interpreted her conversation with Moon Watcher. "He went to speak with El Gato to see if we will be allowed to trade. My guess is that we will see the man himself soon. Moon Watcher said they have don't have much to trade with."

"He doesn't know what we are really after. He's got plenty to trade with, including Tabby."

"At least we know she is alive—and here in this village. She apparently has some freedom to move about the village, although I was surprised that she disappeared."

Wolf said, "Some woman grabbed her arm and led her away. I assume she was not to be seen by us."

"Anyway, she had the good sense not to recognize us. I just hope we can find out where she is staying."

"If they are willing to let us ransom her, it doesn't matter. If not, it will be more difficult to get her out. On the plus side she knows we're here and why. I'm guessing Tabby will find a way to make her whereabouts known."

Jael asked, "We're supposed to be traders. How are you going to shift the subject to ransoming captives?"

"We're something like the renegade Comancheros. We're buying these people as brokers to re-sell in Mexico—or possibly to their families. You had some firsthand knowledge of how the Comancheros did business. I'll let you figure out how to approach it."

"Me? I thought you were in charge here."

"You played the interpreter card to get on this wagon. I don't speak Apache, and it's clumsy talking back and forth through a third party. Besides, you're the law wrangler. If a man's got a lawyer handy, it doesn't make sense to try talking for himself. By the time you finish making your case, you might get a new client out of the deal—the whole Apache nation."

"The thought had crossed my mind, but not this soon. But you are serious about me doing the negotiating?"

"Yep. You can always stop and tell them you need to confer with me at any point. But do what you must. I won't be second-guessing you on this."

She appreciated Wolf's confidence but was not entirely surprised at his decision. He was devoid of the male ego so many men suffered. He respected a woman for what she could do and was intolerant of a female's claim to victimhood. A woman rode with Oliver Wolf as a full partner. Jael was married to someone like that, and that was one reason why she had failed to understand the unfair way Tabby had treated this gifted and exceptional man.

The remaining onlookers began to stir and burst into a chattering that caught Jael's attention. Beyond the throng, she saw Moon Watcher approaching with a tall warrior wearing a buckskin vest that revealed sinewy arms and muscular shoulders and chest and came up not far short of the physical specimen that Wolf presented. This had to be El Gato. Another man a decade or more older than the other two followed. As the assembly part-ed to allow the men to pass through, she noted that the third man was missing his left hand.

When they stepped in front of Wolf and Jael and stopped, Moon Watcher spoke in Apache, "This is El Gato, chief of our band." He nodded toward El Gato. "And counselor, One Hand."

Jael interpreted to Wolf, who raised his hand in a sign of peace but received no response.

She directed her words to El Gato, "I am She Who Speaks. This is my husband, White Wolf." She had decided that spouses traveling together might make more sense to the Apaches and that the lie might prove strategic before the day was out. She would need to inform Wolf of their marriage soon, however.

El Gato offered a disdainful grunt, setting his face in a scowl before speaking. "I know of She Who Speaks. Apaches have joked about our old enemy, the Comanche war chief Quanah, who listened to the words of a woman and treated her with the respect due only a warrior. Perhaps that is why he is now on the white man's reservation."

Jael decided she was not going to tolerate ridicule by the arrogant chief. "The man you mock is now the first chief of all Comanche, not just a band. His people will not starve when winter comes, and soon they will be wealthy. I also know of the warrior Lozen, sister of Victorio, acknowledged chief of the Mimbres—the eastern Chiricahuas. Your people are part of this band. Do you deride Lozen and Victorio also?" He seemed to flinch for an instant at her comment.

"You should be called She Who Talks Too Much."

This time Jael returned a good-natured smile. "Others have told me that."

El Gato nodded. He studied her for several moments, and she had the feeling she was being stripped naked. Then he said, "Moon Watcher said you want to trade. I wonder why we should not just take, but we will talk first. There." He pointed to the tree where they had spotted Tabby and turned and commenced walking toward it.

Jael had no idea how much English any of the Apaches might understand, so she turned to Wolf and said, "Husband, the chief will talk. We are to follow."

Wolf was not the least taken aback. "Wife, the chief seems to be a wise man. I am sure he will see that it will benefit his people to trade with us and would not dishonor his band by harming honest traders."

Wolf and Jael staked out their horses and pack mule nearby. Wolf removed his gun belt and hung his holstered Army Colt on the saddle horn. They left their

Winchesters in the scabbards, but neither abandoned the sheathed knives, which both handled expertly. Jael decided El Gato would be the first to feel her blade at any sign of treachery.

The three Apaches sat in a small semi-circle across from Jael and Wolf when they sat down in the sparse shade of the tree to talk. The other Apaches drifted away, although some remained within hearing, obviously curious about the meeting.

It did not appear that El Gato was going to speak, so Jael initiated the discussion in Apache. "We have many things to offer in trade that will be useful to your people. Pots, blankets, knives, clothes for all ages, some sheepskin coats for winter."

El Gato said, "But no guns?"

"No guns. But we have gold that would allow you to buy whatever you need for your people."

At the mention of gold, El Gato's eyes brightened with interest. "We have very little to trade. Some furs and deerskins, a few robes."

"Horses. We can always find a market for good horses."

"No horses. We have none to spare. We must keep all our horses."

"We would take furs and deerskins in trade, but unless you have many of these things, we could not trade you all the goods on our pack mule and, certainly, no gold."

"The gold we could take, and your trade goods, and we could eat the mule."

"You could, but we came to this place because we heard El Gato was a man of honor. And there are others who know we came here. If we do not return, the word will spread to others that El Gato steals from traders, and you will learn that traders will not deal with you. Even those who sell guns will stay away. Also, our gold is hidden elsewhere. We did not bring it with us. We will bring it here only if you have merchandise to sell or trade. Otherwise, we have located Victorio's village, and we will go there with our trade goods and gold." She had sensed that El Gato looked upon his ally, Victorio, as something of a rival, and she intended to leverage the Apache's envy in her trading.

Jael thought she saw a twinkle in Moon Watcher's eyes, set deeply in his otherwise unreadable face. One Hand's head was turned toward El Gato, awaiting his response. The chief appeared to be pondering her remarks but could not hide his annoyance.

Finally, he spoke. "You will not be harmed if you remain in peace. We will talk more. Do you buy for sale to the Mexicans?"

She hoped this was leading in the direction she suspected. She had not wanted to be the one to initiate talk of purchase of captives. "Yes. We sometimes do, but our contacts there are usually only interested in slaves or captives we have purchased. Those we deal with were Comancheros I encountered while with Quanah. My husband sometimes rode with Comancheros. That is how I met him. The Comanche often conducted business with these people."

"Your husband is not Comanche?"

"No. He is mixed-blood. Cherokee and the white man's Scottish peoples. He was a great warrior in the white man's tribal war between North and South. He came to the Llano Estacada after the war."

El Gato nodded. "Yes, you would have met such traders among the Comanche. You acted as interpreter for transactions with the Comancheros?"

"Yes. I speak many tongues."

"I have heard there is no tongue you cannot speak."

"That is not true, but the Great Spirit endowed me with a gift for languages." Jael figured it would not harm to toss the Great Spirit into the mix. She had found that people of all cultures were quick to recruit the deity to their side of a mission.

El Gato said, "Do you talk in the Mexican tongue?"

"Yes. They speak Spanish. Your name is from that language. 'The Cat.'"

"So you can trade with the Mexicans?"

"Yes. As I said, we have ways."

"We have Navajos to sell."

Now they were making progress. She would need to broach the trade or ransom delicately. If she appeared too eager, the price might go too high, and if she seemed to know too much, El Gato might become suspicious. "We were at Fort Defiance to purchase trade goods and supplies and heard Navajos had been taken captive. There was a white woman, too."

"There is no white woman here. We have a boy, two girls not yet having their moon time, and a young woman not claimed for a wife. Another Navajo woman has become One Hand's wife."

El Gato turned to One Hand and asked if he wanted to sell the woman, and the older warrior said he did not. He also asked One Hand if he would keep the boy, who was apparently the woman's child. The Navajo woman must be Sunrise, Delgado's wife, and the boy, their son, Fears Nothing, Jael thought.

One Hand told El Gato, "The boy is stubborn. He refuses to join the other boys in war games. He insists he is Diné and that he will never be Apache. I think that may be so. His mother tries to make him obey, but he refuses." He lifted the palm of his sole hand outward, exhibiting a scabbed slice running the width of the palm. "We must hide knives from him. Three suns ago, he attacked me and cut my hand when I raised it to defend. I switched his naked buttocks until he bled. He did not cry and is still unrepentant. He has Apache courage, but I do not think he will ever be anything but Navajo. Most his age assimilate quickly. I do not have the patience for this. If I cannot sell him, I will be forced to kill him, and that would displease his mother."

"We will buy this boy," Jael said, "There are men who desire young boys and enjoy those most who resist their advances." She knew that the Apaches would not grasp this concept, any more than her Comanche family did. Male sexual relationships between persons of their own gender were taboo and would be punished or bar participants from leadership. Women discreetly sharing a robe generally did little more than trigger joke-making. Assault of any child, however, brought about the offender's death. She had read that Apaches even went so far as to kill all discovered male homosexuals, with women again being allowed some latitude.

"And you would also take the girls and unclaimed woman?"

"If we can agree upon a fair price." She did not wish to appear too anxious. "I must see the merchandise."

El Gato thought about this and then shrugged and turned to Moon Watcher. "Walks Far speaks the Navajo tongue. See if she will help you gather the trade property and bring them here."

Moon Watcher said, "I can do this." He got up and walked away.

Jael turned to Wolf and explained what had transpired during the negotiations and that Moon Watcher was fetching the young Navajos. "It appears that Delgado's wife is claimed by One Hand. There is no white woman here. No other captives. And I have to pee."

She seized the opportunity to break an uncomfortable silence and spoke to El Gato, "I must relieve myself of water. Can someone show me the waste grounds?"

El Gato gave her an exasperated look. One Hand said, "I will take her there and keep watch."

One Hand led her along the fringes of the village, while Jael's eyes roamed the wickiups scattered about the village. When she reached the waste ground, she winced at the oppressive stink there, remembering that not so many years had passed since she had performed her necessary bodily functions in a similar place among the Comanche. Civilization was spoiling her. She found a dry spot on the rocky surface, dropped her britches to her ankles and squatted. One Hand stood about ten paces distant, not bothering to turn his head away. She didn't care. She was not being devious when she said she had to pee. Wolf seemed to have an iron bladder, and she envied him for that.

When she had finished her task, they headed back to the pine tree bargaining place. This time, she caught sight of Tabby again, standing near a wickiup some twenty-five yards distant. Her friend was looking Jael's way but gave no sign of recognition.

Soon after she settled in to talk again, Jael saw Moon Watcher walking toward the pine tree beside a pretty woman who held a boy's hand, followed by a stick-figured young woman and two girls, one short and the other four or five inches taller. Delgado had told Jael that the girls were twins, though one would never guess from either appearance or behavior. The taller twin was named Red Feather, and her sister was known as Blue Feather. The young woman was called Runs Alone and said to be very quiet and standoffish, a person that some whites would call a loner.

When the party arrived, Moon Watcher said, continuing to speak Apache, "The little one tried to run, but his mother and Walks Far caught him. He may have to be tied if you buy him."

Jael smiled at the boy. His hostile glare softened, but he was not yet surrendering. "Let us bargain for the boy first."

Jael was surprised to find the woman Moon Watcher had referred to as Walks Far spoke some English. "I am Diné. Boy is Fears Nothing." She gave an impish smile. "See why you take. I talk boy. Tell Fears Nothing why go with you. He want see Smokey."

Smokey. Tabby's gelding. This woman was sending her a message from Tabby, perhaps a signal that Walks Far was a friend. She had declared she was Navajo, probably a captive herself at one time. Like herself, who had become Comanche, this woman had likely been adopted by the Apaches years ago and adapted to another life. But also like the Jewish Jael Chernik, who had been abducted at age fourteen after her parents were murdered, Walks Far had been old enough to retain prior language skills and had not entirely abandoned her original identity.

"I understand Smokey," Jael replied.

Walks Far gave a barely perceptible nod.

Jael addressed El Gato in Apache, "What will you take for the boy?"

El Gato leaned over to Moon Watcher and spoke something too softly for her to hear. Moon Watcher apparently had some understanding of money and purchase values and was trying to explain equivalents in terms of rifles and other goods. Finally, El Gato said, "We want one thousand dollars in gold."

"Too much. You should pay us to take this wild one off your hands."

"We can kill him or sell to other trader."

Jael turned to Wolf. "He wants a thousand dollars."

"With Cal's money, we have plenty to work with, but if we let this thief rob us on the boy, he will raise the ante on the others. We need to get rid of the trade goods. See if he will take everything on the mule for the boy. We have about six hundred dollars invested there."

"I'll see what I can do." She spoke again to El Gato. "I was going to offer five hundred dollars for the boy, but the trade goods on the mule are worth much more than that. You may have all the trade goods for the boy. This way your people will see immediate benefits from the trade."

El Gato consulted again with Moon Watcher. Soon he turned back to Jael and said, "Done."

The negotiations continued for another hour, and eventually the twins were purchased for one thousand dollars each and the young woman sold for fifteen hundred dollars. El Gato reluctantly agreed to include two horses in the purchase. Jael made another attempt to purchase Sunrise, but One Hand would not consider an offer. She could not attempt to bargain for Tabitha without calling El Gato a liar, which risked costing them the entire trade.

She asked Wolf, "How do we make the exchange? We must return to North Star to pick up the gold in order to make payment."

"See if they will let us take the prisoners with us. They can send several riders with us to collect payment."

"He won't buy it, but I'll see what I can do."

"If we are going to meet to make the exchange, it has got to be at the base of the trail just before the climb starts. We don't want to ride into the village again and risk being swarmed. North Star can stay back and keep an eye out for ambush when you and I meet to complete the exchange."

"I understand." Switching to Apache, she put forth Wolf's proposal, which was immediately rejected.

El Gato offered a counter-proposal. "Boy goes. She Who Speaks stays with other Navajo prisoners. When gold comes, you and the others go."

Wolf was not going to like this, but Jael immediately saw an opportunity. If she stayed behind, she had a chance of communicating with Tabby. Perhaps the woman Walks Far would help. The woman was obviously not hostile, but Jael had no way of knowing if the congeniality went so far as to assist captives with escape from the village.

"I will stay," Jael said.

When she told Wolf of the bargain, he said, "No. I don't like this. Tell him, we will leave the boy and come back with the gold and meet at the base of the mountain."

He finally relented, however, after she persuaded him of the soundness of the strategy in contacting Tabby. Speaking barely above a whisper, she had said, "Tabby needs to know where Cal and Delgado are, and we've got to find out how we can help her escape this place," Jael pointed out. "And I lived many years with the Comanche. It doesn't frighten me to stay here. El Gato has unintentionally given us the key to the back door."

Wolf sighed. "Does Josh ever win an argument with you?"

"I don't remember. He might have once."

An hour later, the mule was unpacked, and Jael watched as Wolf, followed by Fears Nothing astride the mule bareback headed down the trail leading from the mesa. Her mount, she had learned, was being held hostage with the owner. She figured Wolf and the boy should hit foothills not far from camp with another hour of sunlight remaining. When she turned away, she was startled to find that Walks Far had quietly slipped up beside her.

"She Who Speaks come eat my wickiup. Take to sleep place after."

"Thank you. Can I see Tabby?"

"See Ta-Bee when safe. Not now."

Chapter 24

DELGADO LED CAL to the lower level of the canyon where the stream widened and spilled out and rushed southward toward lush grasslands beyond. Cow country, Cal thought. No wonder the Mexicans wanted the Apaches out of there and had not been able to resist amassing great haciendas in the area. Unfortunately, according to Delgado, most within a day's ride were now vacated with most buildings burned out and remaining cattle and horses turned wild.

The walk over the rugged mountainous terrain had been challenging with only a few occasional deer and goat paths to offer breaks from the treacherous footing on the slopes. Bringing horses would have been difficult and hiding them from Apache scouts and sentries impossible. The Apache village-hideaway was virtually impregnable from the west, and Cal took Delgado at his word that the east was equally safe from attack. If they took the same route out of the canyon, they would not be chased down by riders on horseback. But could they outrun pursuing Apaches afoot? Better not to be placed in that position.

The two men were hidden behind a jagged stone outcropping curtained by several small cottonwoods clinging to its edge. As their eyes followed the ribbon of water to its source up the steep canyon that framed it and into the mountaintops, Cal spoke in a near whisper, "The damn canyon twists and turns like a crawling rattler. Can't see what's around the next curve. Good, if you're the one waiting for somebody. Not so good, if some devil Apache is waiting for you."

Delgado said, "There are trails on both sides of the stream. East trail is three or four horses wide. A war party can get up and down fast on that. Other is single-horse, maybe just used for walking."

"That one's got a kind of slope for fifteen feet or so above it. Lot of sage and pines on the grade. Think we could take the high ground—at least as far as it allows? I ain't anxious to walk on moving rock again, but I'd rather be looking down at an Apache warrior than direct in his beady eyes."

Delgado said, "It makes sense. Of course, they could have a lookout posted on that same high ground, and with the sliding rock, we would never sneak up on anybody."

"We got to work our way up closer to the village and see what's going on there. Can't get Little Sis and your wife and boy out if we don't know where they've got them." He stopped abruptly. "Listen. Hoofbeats coming from the south, Not many but more than a few."

They hunkered down behind the boulders and trees on the outcropping and waited. Soon five mounted Apache warriors appeared at the canyon's mouth and headed up the wide trail on the other side of the stream that climbed the steep incline toward the mesa. Cal heard a man call what he assumed was a greeting to the riders and a flurry of voices answering.

"There's one close by we got to take out," Cal said. He looked skyward. "A few hours past high noon. I'm thinking we take a page from this El Gato's book and make our move after sundown—but not much. That suit you?"

Delgado said, "I don't have a better idea. He will not mistake us for Apaches in the sunlight. And a man your size won't be taken for an Apache anytime."

"Let's think on this a spell. Got nothin' but time anyhow."

Late afternoon, they ate the last of their jerky and biscuits. "Down to berries and roots," Cal remarked. "Sure as hell hope you know your wild grub."

"We will not starve, I promise, but you will not be happy with the menu."

As the sun slipped behind the mountaintop, Cal and Delgado removed their moccasins and rolled the legs of their britches up to their knees. They moved out from behind their cover and slid quietly as loose shale would allow down the slope, landing only a few yards from the stream. They waded into the stream, possible sacks slung over their shoulders and Winchesters held high enough to avoid the water. The impact from the racing waters leaping over the rocks tested their footwork, and Cal almost toppled backward upon taking his first step into the icy rapids. Rolling up their britches' legs had been a futile exercise, for at its deepest the water swirled around the thighs of Cal's long legs and reached Delgado's buttocks.

When they stumbled onto the east bank, Cal and Delgado hurried across the trail and into the brush and trees beyond. As he rolled down the sopped legs of his buckskin britches and pulled on his moccasins, Cal began to shiver from the cold visited upon him by the frigid water and rapidly cooling night, but he quickly shook it off. He had work to do.

He studied the trail and the canyon walls that loomed above it. As they had already guessed, there was no way to get above the lookout who was likely perched on the trail ahead. There was no choice but to move forward with the original plan. Cal's fingers caressed the hilt of the Bowie knife nestled in the sheath snuggled against his hip. No gunfire, or the party was over.

"Ready?" Cal whispered to Delgado.

"Yes."

Delgado moved out ahead of Cal and onto the trail and then started walking slowly up the slope. Cal waited a bit and then fell in about twenty paces behind. It took about ten minutes to reach the twist in the trail where the Apache riders had disappeared and where they had heard the greeting of the presumed sentry. They hoped the warrior was not there, but they could not risk his presence. Before he made the turn, Delgado set his rifle down on the trail's edge and fell to his knees. He began to crawl and started moaning as if mortally wounded. When he turned the corner, he was to drop to his belly and to continue to inch his way forward. Hopefully, this would bring any guard from hiding, and curiosity and uncertainty would quell a premature squeeze of any rifle trigger.

Cal thought Delgado's performance was good enough for the stage of the Teatro Santa Fe, the town's cultural center operated by actress-entrepreneur Jessica Chandler. Delgado disappeared and his moaning softened, a signal that there was company on the trail. Cal quickened his pace and set his own Winchester down next to Delgado's, slipping the Bowie from its sheath. Before he turned the corner, he stopped and waited.

"Ayuda," Delgado choked out. Help. The signal.

Cal whipped around the trail's twist to find an Apache warrior standing over Delgado, poking the downed man with his rifle barrel. His eyes widened when he saw Cal barreling his way, and he started to raise his rifle. Too late. Cal ran him over like a charging bull, and the weapon dropped from his hands before he was flattened against the stone trail. Cal was on him, driving the big knife into the Apache's belly and ripping it upward, before rolling him over, latching his powerful arm about the warrior's neck and snapping it to assure silence.

Delgado jumped to his feet and helped Cal drag the body to the edge of the stream. They heaved the corpse to mid-channel, and Cal nodded with satisfaction as he watched the dead Apache bouncing in the rush of water on its journey downstream. Of course, the body could get hung up on brush or rocks at any point, but he judged there was a fair chance the trip could amount to miles. It had been their only option. Hiding the body nearby would not have helped for long. The buzzards would have given up the secret in the morning, and discovery of the dead warrior would have confirmed the presence of enemies.

Cal thought it unlikely that the canyon entrance would be watched by a single sentinel. There was most certainly at least one more, probably much further up the narrowing canyon nearer the village site.

After retrieving their rifles, with some reluctance they crossed the stream again, Cal thinking the narrow trail along the west canyon wall would reduce the likelihood of running headlong into Apaches descending the mountain. It seemed to Cal that any lookout would still be posted on the east side as well, given the wider trail and a wall broken up with numerous cracks and crevices adaptable for concealing a man with a weapon. Their hope was that they would see the guard, and one would distract while the other crossed the stream and worked up behind the Apache. Cal and Delgado moved stealthily up the trail, Cal taking the lead this time with Delgado trailing some distance behind. The hikers shifted into the shadows whenever they could dodge the moonlight, fighting off the urge to hurry as their eyes searched the walls across the stream and the trail ahead. An hour later, Cal found himself increasingly uneasy, pleased he had not encountered a challenge but doubting entry to the mesa where the village was located would be so thinly guarded.

Justification came to his doubts when a boulder-like force crushed into his back and searing pain struck his ribs. Cal fell forward, his face crunching into the shale-covered trail. He felt the hand cup his chin to yank his head back for the death cut, and instinctively he raised up his torso and rolled, his powerful shoulders lifting the Apache warrior like a bucking horse. The Apache tumbled off his back, and Cal slipped the Bowie from its sheath as he started to right himself and face his attacker. Unnecessary. Delgado had a hold on the warrior's hair, and blood was spewing over his knife blade as it tore through the soft flesh of the Apache's throat.

Delgado rolled the attacker's body over the rise above the stream, launching it into the rushing water. Cal hoped the corpse would catch up with the other warrior's many miles from this place.

He leaned back against the canyon wall and traced his fingers over the wound carved when the knife blade pierced his buckskin shirt and sliced into his rib cage. He felt the slick, warm blood and the gaping flesh. He sighed, "Damn. Didn't need this. I never saw the son-of-a-bitch. He came out of nowhere."

By this time, Delgado was at his side, pulling up Cal's torn shirt to reveal the wound and then probing with his fingers. Cal flinched at the sharp pain but said nothing. The Navajo unsheathed his knife, peeled off his cotton shirt and began slicing off the bottom ridge of the garment.

Delgado spoke softly. "He must have been flattened out on the ledge that juts out over the edge of the trail here. I saw something raise up and at first thought it was an animal. Then he lunged and just dropped on you. I couldn't fire without waking the whole village up canyon. So I just ran to catch up."

"You made it in time. That's what counts. I owe you."

"You owe me nothin'. I think you would have won out on your own." Delgado rinsed the wound with his canteen and tried to compress the cut by wrapping the strip from his shirt around Cal's chest before realizing it was too short to span the big man's torso. He sliced another strip from his shirt and tied the two together to make the wrap. As he finished knotting the crude bandage, he said, "You are not going to bleed out, but the wound is going to be seeping for a good spell. It needs to be stitched, but I can't do that--not here anyway."

"Lucky I'm alive to feel the pain. Still can't believe the bastard jumped me like that. He must not of saw you coming behind me."

"I just came around the turn in the trail when I caught sight of him. Apaches are like ghosts. They can hide behind a blade of grass in full sunlight and be ten feet from you, and your eyes still won't pick them up."

"Before this happened, I wouldn't have believed you, but now I half do. Tabby's going to give me some gaff about this. Speaking of my crazy little sis, we ain't going to help nobody with me sitting here on my ass." Cal got up on his knees, and leaning against the canyon wall, clambered to his feet.

The injured ribs complained with each step, but Cal stepped aside and allowed Delgado to take the lead and struggled to keep up the pace, which he knew the Navajo had slowed for his benefit. Soon Delgado came upon a deer path that led off the trail and into a fissure in the mountainside. He paused and pointed to the branch-off from the main trail.

Cal studied the break in the wall. Wide enough at the opening for one man to walk through with arms spread, he figured. Too dark to tell where it led or how deep it went. "Critters wouldn't be stomping a path to a dead end," he said. "Let's see where it takes us."

Delgado nodded his approval and disappeared into the stone wall. The path continued a steep climb and the only light that thwarted pitch-blackness in the passageway came from the ribbon of stars that could be seen by looking upward between the craggy walls. The corridor narrowed as they moved higher but never threatened to obstruct their passage. The pain in Cal's ribs grew as ascent steepened, forcing him to scramble upward on hands and knees. Breathing heavily, he was relieved to see Delgado break into moonlight ahead of him.

When he joined his comrade, he was glad to see they had emerged on a patch of relatively flat ground at the mountain's base overlooking the mesa where the Apache village sat. There was good cover here with gooseberry bushes and buckbrush scattered about and small aspen and pine trees clinging to the rocky surface.

Cal could make out the shadowy outlines of wickiups on the mesa, which he noted dropped off gradually to meadows where horses grazed. The path they had taken continued toward the mesa and forked off toward the meadows that deer would claim when the Apaches and their horses were absent. He calculated that if they had stuck to the main path, he and Delgado would have ended up at the meadows, where they probably would have run into a few more Apaches guarding the remuda.

The men sat down to ponder their next move. "This might be a good spot to dig in for now," Cal said. "Don't think we could do much better for seein' things unless we walked right into the village."

"And if we walk into the village, we'd just as well lower our heads and surrender our scalps. I agree."

"I doubt if Apaches take this branch of the trail much. Too steep. Main trail would've been a gradual climb that takes you right into the meadow and then on up to the village. Of course, most Apaches likely take the big trail on the opposite side of the creek, anyway. Appears they end up the same place."

"We can't do anything till morning," Delgado said. "Then, all we can do is watch and be ready. I don't like that we do not know what Wolf is doing at the north entrance."

"For now, he just wants us to wait and be ready. He wants to make first move. We'll give him a few days, and, if nothing happens, we'll do something on our own. For all we know, the others could be dead or hightailing it by now. And I ain't leaving this place till I know Tabby got away or I got her with me."

"And I will not leave without Sunrise and Fears Nothing."

"Then we understand each other."

Chapter 25

THE KID WAS tougher than a young grizzly, Wolf thought. Or just plain stubborn. Sometimes the line between tough and stubborn could be blurry. Wolf and Fears Nothing had nearly completed the trek down the narrow mountainside trail that led away from the north side of the Apache enclave. Wolf had assumed the boy would ride behind him on Owl during their trip to rendezvous with North Star. But the twelve-year-old had refused and insisted he would have his own mount. Thus, the boy was riding the mule and seemed happy enough straddled bareback on the docile critter. The mule was accustomed to following a horse without protest or complaint, and the arrangement appeared to be working well enough. The boy maneuvered the animal efficiently enough with improvised straps on the halter.

Wolf was at first surprised to discover the boy spoke near perfect English. Then he remembered that Delgado's English was nearly flawless, better grammatically than that of most whites who occupied or frequented the southwestern United States. He suspected the boy's mother spoke the tongue as well. Regardless, Fears Nothing had no interest in idle conversation. He was mostly silent, but that suited Wolf just fine. He generally preferred a world of silence and spoke sparingly to all but those with whom he was close. Tabby sometimes had him babbling, he thought. But they could both share a room for hours without speaking to the other, lost in their separate thoughts or Tabby writing and Wolf sketching. He had missed those companionable silent times, where mere presence of the other brought contentment. He could not be certain they would ever share those moments again. But, for now, all that mattered was to bring Tabby out of the Apache village alive and well.

Two mounted warriors waited at the juncture where the mountain trail met more level terrain. Their faces were neither hostile nor friendly, but they were not especially threatening. Wolf nodded but got no response. As he swung Owl onto the path that led through trees and undergrowth and into the foothills, Fears Nothing and the mule fell in behind.

Wolf tossed a glance over his shoulder and saw that the warriors were following. It miffed him, but he was certain El Gato had ordered the shadowing, and there was nothing he could do to stop it short of killing the two, which he did not consider useful. Not yet, anyway. It was turning dusky now, but North Star's camp was only two hours' distant. That assumed he had not been attacked and the horses and gold taken, which would necessitate a new strategy, after he disposed of the Apaches who trailed him now.

Fears Nothing reined up beside him, saying nothing as they rode side by side for a time. Finally, the boy spoke. "I do not like those coyotes following us."

Wolf replied, "I don't like it either, but there is nothing we can do about it"

"There is something. We can kill them."

"Yes. But there is no purpose to that. Not now."

"They are Apaches. That is enough purpose." He pointed at Wolf's rifle cradled in the saddle scabbard. "Let me take this, and I will kill them."

"You can handle a rifle?"

"Yes. I shoot better than many Navajo warriors and better than any Apache warrior."

"Well, I'm not going to give you my rifle. I think we have an extra at our campsite. I will let you carry a rifle, if you promise not to use it unless I say so."

Fears Nothing was quiet, apparently pondering the condition Wolf had imposed. Finally, the boy said, "I promise."

Darkness had fully settled in by the time they reached North Star's camp. There was no fire, a necessary precaution with Apaches currently flooding the area. The Apache watchmen fell back and reined in their horses as Wolf and the boy rode up the ridge to high ground and broke through the trees and undergrowth surrounding the camp clearing. There was no sign of North Star, but Wolf could see a few of the horses staked out downstream.

Wolf did not call out, but spoke in a soft voice, "North Star. It's Wolf and a young guest. The two outriders are Apaches, but I don't think they are a threat."

North Star stepped out of the trees, raising his hand in greeting. "I recognized your horse and the mule. I was worried about the wolves out there. Who's your friend?"

Wolf dismounted, and Fears Nothing slid off the mule's back. Wolf said, "This is Fears Nothing, Delgado's son. He's what I got for the ransom price so far."

"Where is my rifle?" Fears Nothing demanded.

"Pleased to meet you, too," North Star replied.

Wolf said, "The young man claims he can handle a rifle. I told him he could use our extra if he promised not to fire it unless I told him to."

North Star looked at the boy dubiously. "Whatever you say. I can get it out. Bullets, too?"

"Yeah, I guess. Maybe we can come up with a little sack of bullets to tie on to that cord that holds up his breechclout."

"We can get him outfitted, I think. But where is Jael?"

"With the Apaches."

"You traded her for him?" North Star asked.

"Well, it's more complicated than that." Wolf gave North Star the details of the bargain Jael had negotiated.

"So, if the Apaches keep their part of the bargain, everybody goes free but this boy's mother and cousin Tabby?"

"That's right. Of course, El Gato doesn't even admit to having Tabby."

"So what do we do about her?"

"I think that's why Jael was so quick to agree to stay behind. She will try to work out an escape plan with Tabby and then tell us what they've planned when she leaves with us and the ransomed captives."

"She is crazy like Tabby?"

"A bit. Maybe that's why they're such good friends."

"So what do you want me to do?"

"We will head back to the Apache village in the morning. I hate to, but we'll have to take Fears Nothing with us. We can't leave him here alone. We'll take all the horses. Can't leave them behind either. We might need them. Or Apaches will come along and help themselves to good horseflesh. I will stuff enough gold in my saddlebags to pay the ransom price and ride back into the village alone and complete the deal. With any luck, Jael and I will ride out with the captives."

"What about me and the kid?"

"I want you to wait at the base of the mountain, back in the trees near where the trail heads up the mountainside. Be ready to cover us if El Gato changes his mind. I think he'll keep his word unless he figures out we're up to something with Sunrise and Tabby."

"And the two who are following you?"

"They may follow me on up the trail to the village. If they stay in your vicinity, just keep an eye on them. If they make a move on you, use your rifle. We'll just have to ad lib if that happens. There will likely be a lot of that tomorrow. I just hope Cal and Delgado made it and are in place."

"And your two Apache wolves? Can we trust them to keep to themselves tonight?"

"No. We'll keep watch in shifts. I don't think they'll move in if they know we're keeping an eye out."

Fears Nothing stepped between the men. "My rifle?"

Chapter 26

JAEL SHARED A meal with Walks Far and her children, helping roast what was obviously chunks of beef loin on forked sticks over the fire while the woman nursed her baby. Beans also boiled in a small pot, and cornbread warmed on stones near the flames. The Apaches were far from starving here. This was nothing like the final weeks of starvation the Kwahadi had endured before their sad trek from the Great Plains to the reservation at Fort Sill. But she knew the feasting would not last. Hunger and deprivation lurked not far away, and the soldiers would eventually root them out and overwhelm with sheer numbers and superior weapons.

The women spoke of mundane things while they ate, Jael telling of her time with the Comanche and Walks Far explaining how she, of the Diné, came to be at this place. Jael was surprised to learn that their lives had traveled very similar paths. Walks Far also mentioned that her husband, Moon Watcher, was meeting with El Gato and hinted that there was dissent within the band. Some, including Walks Far, wished to return to the reservation. This life was death, she insisted. At least on the reservation, whatever misery might be imposed by the whites, there would be hope, if not for her, for her children. A wise woman, Jael thought.

After they ate, Walks Far led Jael to the wickiup where the soon-to-be ransomed Navajos were staying. The three had returned following negotiations and now knelt in front of the lodge, skinning and gutting small game, including rabbits, squirrels and several large rattlesnakes. The young woman and two girls looked up expectantly, as Walks Far and Jael approached.

Walks Far spoke Navajo to the young captives, and they turned happy faces toward Jael. However, Runs Alone's smile was tentative and her eyes reflected some skepticism. Apparently, Walks Far was talking about Jael. Being multi-lingual, she had become accustomed to understanding almost any conversation she encountered and did not like the exclusion. This made her even more determined to add the Navajo language to her catalog.

Walks Far turned to Jael. "I tell them you called She Who Speaks. They hear talk with El Gato but not know what happen. I say you take home. You sleep here."

"Do they speak any English?"

"Runs Alone talk English good, I think. Red Feather, Blue Feather, only little."

Jael decided to confront Walks Far with her most urgent concern. "If all goes as agreed, I will leave with Runs Alone and the girls when White Wolf brings the ransom gold tomorrow. I must talk to Tabby. Can you help me?"

"El Gato say you stay here. Sun go away, Ta-Bee come. I go now."

Walks Far disappeared quickly into the maze of wickiups, pole tripods and drying racks, leaving Jael alone with her new charges. She got down on one knee. "If you have another knife, I can help."

The girls did not seem to understand, but Runs Alone answered, "We have no others. The Apache pig who gives us work counts all knives when the work is done and takes them away. She knows I would keep one if I could and kill with it when I decided it was time. Blue Feather has difficulty with this work. You may use her knife and she will hang the meat and scrape the skins with the sharp stones."

"I would be glad to help. Perhaps we can talk while we work."

Jael joined the skinning crew, and only a few minutes later a squat woman with a scowling face showed up with a wild turkey hanging from her hand which was clutched about its neck. She shot Jael an angry glare and tossed the bird's carcass at her. Jael dodged the missile and its feathers scraped her face as it plopped to the ground behind her. The Apache woman whirled and stomped off.

"I don't think she likes me," Jael commented.

Runs Alone said, "Turtle does not like anyone. They say she is worse since her husband took a younger wife. But she is probably angry because she heard you are taking us from the village. She collects the bounty of the hunts and assigns the skinning and butchering to others. What she cannot give to others, she must do herself. She will miss her slaves."

"So that's why you have so much to do here. You are like a village butcher shop?"

"I have read about butcher shops. Yes, I guess you could say that."

"You have obviously enjoyed a good education."

"I started at the government school established near the Bosque Redondo and continued at the Fort Defiance school. My father died during the Long Walk, but my mother insisted that I get an education in the white schools. To allow me to attend school, we even lived near Fort Defiance where she did laundry and cleaned residences for the officers. I had wonderful teachers. Miss Lawson, my favorite teacher, married a soldier who is now stationed at Fort Riley in Kansas. She invited me to live with them and attend the Kansas State Agricultural College in Manhattan. I would learn things I could bring back to the Diné reservation. But now I don't know."

"You are leaving this place. There is no reason you cannot continue with your schooling."

"I will make no plans until we have returned to the Diné. My mother is of the Hawk clan, and we were visiting relatives at the clan's village when the attack came. We have not lived among the clan for many years. In some ways I understand the whites better than I do my own people. My heart is split."

Jael understood. Some days she was a white lawyer. Others she was still Comanche. She would try to help this young woman carve her own path through life.

Turtle delivered no more game for butchering, and when all the carcasses had been processed and the skins stretched on racks, the meat cuts were packed on a pole stretcher and delivered by Runs Alone and Red Feather to Turtle at her wickiup. When they returned, the Navajos and Jael roasted meat from one of the rattlesnakes they had been allowed to hold back for their labor. Jael had enjoyed rattlesnake during her life among the Comanche and savored the delicacy. There was no other food to accompany the meal, however, and Jael noted that her new friends did not share the more varied meals ingested by their captors.

TABITHA'S STOMACH FLUTTERED with excitement at the thought of meeting up with her dearest friend. She could not believe Jael was in the village, less than three minutes distant at this moment. She was at once happy and fearful, delighted at the prospect of seeing her friend again and afraid for Jael's life. The sun had mostly crawled over the mountaintops now, but she decided to wait for darkness to fully settle in before she sneaked through the village to the wickiup where Jael was staying.

If El Gato visited tonight, and she could only assume he would, he would not slip into the wickiup until very late. The chiefs and senior warriors were in council this evening, and the talk almost always extended for hours. He might, or might not, stop at the wickiup he shared with Cactus Bloom and their children first, but he seemed to be doing this less lately. Why should a war chief explain his whereabouts to a mere woman? Tabitha smiled when she thought of El Gato's reluctance to confront Cactus Bloom. She was a formidable woman.

But Tabitha considered herself no less formidable, and tonight she felt more confident because she had retrieved her skinning knife, slid it into the crude buckskin sheath she had fashioned and hid it in her lodge. El Gato no longer conducted searches when he made his visits, seemingly confident Tabitha was accepting him as her destiny and becoming an obedient wife. She suspected her pregnancy had much to do with his unjustified sureness. Why would a woman seek to escape the father of her child? She thought that in El Gato's mind she needed him now to provide for her and his Apache baby.

When she stepped out of her wickiup, she took the routes less traveled as she weaved through the village, but she walked with shoulders back and head held high. Most no longer thought of her as a prisoner here and would not give much thought to an encounter unless she exhibited a guilty demeanor. As she approached the captives' wickiup, she cast a few furtive glances about and saw no one looking her way. Quickly, she ducked and eased through the wickiup's entry flap. There was no fire to cast light about the interior, and she would be nearly blind until her eyes adjusted.

She started when she felt a pair of arms surround her and pull her close but instantly sensed they belonged to her friend. "Jael, I can't believe you are here. You and Oliver both. It's a dream."

They embraced at length before they eased onto the robe spread out on the floor and sat. She could make out the shadowy forms of the three Navajo captives now, sitting silently on the opposite side of the wickiup.

Jael said, "When Cal sent word, Oliver prepared to leave immediately. I invited myself to join him. He did not like it, but when I told him I spoke a fair amount of Apache, he surrendered."

"But now your life goes on at the whim of El Gato. You never should have stayed here."

"It was the only way we could communicate with you. El Gato did not admit you were here. You were not offered for ransom, and we had to pretend we didn't know of your presence in the village. We would never leave without you. Oliver has a plan, but it's very dangerous. How closely are you watched?"

"Not so much as when I first came here. I don't know how much Walks Far told you."

"What do you mean?"

"Did she tell you I am El Gato's wife—as far as he is concerned?"

"No. She didn't say a word."

"That's like her. She's very discreet. She probably thought it was my place to tell you, if I wanted you to know."

"You are not his wife in the sense you intend to spend the rest of your life with him?"

"Of course not. I never consented, and any marriage would be invalid under territorial law. I am not a lawyer, but I know that much. Besides, I am his second wife, so I guess that makes him a bigamist of sorts."

"My head is spinning."

"There's more. I'm with child."

Dead silence. "Oliver's?" Jael asked in a near whisper.

"No. Impossible."

"Oh, my God. For once I don't know what to say."

"It complicates things. For one thing, as much as I hate El Gato, it is difficult for me to think of killing my child's father."

"You planned to kill El Gato?"

"I have a knife hidden in my lodge for that purpose. I am capable of a kill with a single strike. You know that. I could make myself a widow in a matter of seconds."

"You won't have to kill him if Oliver's plan works out."

"Tell me about the plan."

"You must get word to Sunrise, Delgado's wife."

"Walks Far can do that."

"You have a lot of trust in her."

"I've learned that sometimes we must trust. She is Navajo."

"She told me."

"She will help with the escape so long as Moon Watcher is not endangered. She says if I can break out of the camp, she can keep him from joining any warriors who pursue. There is already a crack in his relationship with El Gato. A break is near, I think."

"I hope you are right. Oliver says you and Sunrise must leave the village by the south passageway tomorrow while the exchange of gold and the captives is taking place. He will make this take as long as possible to give you time. Hopefully, most eyes will be on the exchange, and he expects many of the warriors will be watching the north entrance. El Gato may be worried that Oliver will return with soldiers."

"Sunrise and I can meet at the stream to collect water or bathe. El Gato won't care so long as I am out of sight when Oliver comes back. He would not be pleased to find that you and I have spoken. Fortunately, he doesn't suspect any connection between us."

"Can you find the trail that takes you out the southern route?"

"Oh, yes. It is obvious and heavily traveled. I worry about the lookouts there. I have my Henry but no cartridges. The remuda is near the south canyon. I always thought we might catch mounts there."

"You will need to leave on foot. The routes to Arizona or New Mexico territories by horseback are too limited and swarming with Apaches, according to Delgado. But I haven't told you that, with any luck, Cal and Delgado will be waiting for you to lead you to our meeting place."

"Cal's at the south exit?" Tabitha felt a surge of confidence. She had never anticipated Oliver's appearance so far from Santa Fe. She had doubted he was even aware of her dilemma, but she had held fast to the thought that her brother would never abandon her to the Apaches. Not while he breathed. "How do we find him? I take that back. A stupid question. He will find us. We've just got to make tracks out of this place and leave the rest to Cal."

They talked about details for a short time but agreed there was no way to write a script for the escape. The obstacles they anticipated would likely not be the ones they faced. The challenge would be to react to those spontaneous and potentially lethal conflicts that could not possibly be foreseen.

When Tabitha rose to return to her lodge, she shared a hug with her friend before she stepped out into the brisk night air. As she walked back to her wickiup, she felt so much had been unsaid between them. She was overwhelmed almost to tears when she thought of those who had taken on the mission to rescue her from the consequences of her own foolhardiness—Cal, Oliver, Jael. Her cousin, North Star. And, of course, new friends like Walks Far and Delgado. She was so rich with family and friends. And love. She vowed she would never again take such riches for granted.

Much later, El Gato visited. She struggled to feign enthusiasm for what would be their final intimacy. He seemed preoccupied and hurried, so she hoped he did not notice her half-hearted effort to pleasure him. Thankfully, he departed quickly and did not remain overnight.

After El Gato left, Tabitha gathered the few things she would take with her, including knife and buckskins, which she would carry in a coyote-hide bag until she could change. She dropped an ample supply of jerky she had scavenged into the bag. She picked up her beloved Henry rifle and caressed the stock and barrel before setting it down. Time to say goodbye. She could not be burdened by a weapon she could not use during this race for her life.

She lay down on the robe, anticipating a sleepless night. But sleep quickly caught her unaware, pulling her into a deep slumber that did not release her till sunrise.

Chapter 27

WOLF, ASTRIDE HIS big stallion, followed by North Star and the boy, Fears Nothing, neared the hidden path that led to the trail that snaked up the mountainside to the Apache stronghold. Fears Nothing, now armed with a Winchester and bag of cartridges, had been quick to reclaim the mule as his mount, the other pack mule and Cal's and Delgado's horses and the spares trailed behind on a lead rope. The dust kicked up by the horses of the two Apache chaperones signaled they were not far behind. The string of horses worried Wolf some. They could slow an escape, but they might be needed. And he could not willingly forfeit the mounts to the Apaches. He had decided he could cut the animals free if they impeded evasion of pursuers.

Wolf reined Owl into the brush and trees that shielded the path. As they neared the main trail, the horse nickered, telling him there was another horse ahead. He signaled a halt to the others before kneeing the stallion forward for a look. He was not pleased with what he saw. Where the path hooked up with the trail, three mounted Apaches stood watch, one armed with a rifle and the other two with bows clutched in their hands.

He pondered the meaning of the greeting party. It made a certain sense. El Gato would likely be concerned that Wolf would return with unwelcome visitors such as soldiers or a small army of scalp hunters. The stronghold was virtually unassailable from this side, however. He decided he had no choice but to assume that the warriors' presence amounted to no more than routine watchfulness. He did not like the idea, though, of leaving North Star and Fears Nothing at the trail's base to face the stacked odds should shooting erupt.

Wolf reined the stallion into a tight turnaround and returned to his comrades. North Star looked at him questioningly.

Wolf said, "At least three Apaches ahead and two coming up behind. We're going to tie all the horses except Owl in the trees off the path and hope the devils don't make off with them. I think they're too busy to go for the horses just yet. After we do that, bring your guns and ammunition and walk behind Owl and onto the main trail.

There is a little landing about a hundred yards up, and they'll have a lookout posted there, so you should drop off the trail before then. There are at least two spots where the trail widens before we get that far. Pick one and set up with rifles ready. The trail's too narrow for a rush, so if they come for you, it will be like shooting turkeys."

North Star asked, "What if they fall in behind us?"

"Keep an eye out and let me know if they try it. We'll stop and aim our rifles. They'll get the message. If we make the trail without a run-in, we will hold the cards until I come back down with the ladies."

"When can I kill Apaches?" Fears Nothing asked.

"Only when North Star says so. Everybody's lives depend on you doing what you're told. Understand?"

"Understand."

The kid's involvement made Wolf edgy. He did not count on the boy for any help, but he did not have a clue what else to do with him.

The horses tied, Wolf started the parade, leading Owl into the clearing where the three Apaches waited. The warriors looked at each other with evident puzzlement as the visitors walked by with seeming disinterest. Wolf kept his right hand within quick reach of his Colt in case one of the Indians made a hostile move. He figured he could easily take down two before they did any harm.

The Apaches watched as Wolf's party started the ascent. It appeared they had no instructions to follow.

Wolf breathed a sigh of relief before he tossed a look over his shoulder and saw that their two old friends had closed the gap and were moving their horses onto the trail. Fortunately, North Star saw the Apaches, too, and when they hit the first widening of the trail signaled Fears Nothing that they would set up there. Wolf was pleased that they had fair cover behind boulder fragments there and noted that with rifle barrels pointed their way, the two Apaches reined in. The point of a gun was universal sign language.

Wolf mounted Owl and pushed him on up the trail. As he had assumed, he passed two Apache guards on his way to the mesa top but received no challenge. When he finally rode over the rim, he observed a gathering near the pine tree where they had met the day previous. Of course, El Gato had been informed of Wolf's approach before he even started the climb to the mesa. Wolf nudged the stallion in that direction. As he neared the group, he was pleased to see that Jael was there, holding the reins of her bay gelding and that two respectable-looking mounts bearing Apache saddle pads were nearby, not far from the ransomed captives.

El Gato waited near the tree, again accompanied by One Hand and Moon Watcher. Another half dozen warriors stood some ten paces back but did not seem especially threatening. Wolf dismounted and removed the saddle bags from the stallion. First, he walked over and spoke softly to Jael. "Did they return your Winchester and ammunition?"

"They did."

"Tell your Navajo friends to get mounted and ready to ride while we pay the ransom."

"Okay. We don't have time to waste."

Wolf carried the saddlebags over to the Apache leaders and dropped them on the ground at El Gato's feet. They engaged in a stare-down that neither won until Jael joined him. "Ask him if he wants me to count the money out," he said.

Jael and the war chief exchanged words in Apache until she turned to Wolf and said, "He wants you to count out the money. Moon Watcher will judge if you have the right amount."

"Damn it. I want to get moving." He knelt, lifted the saddlebags, and spilled the gold out on the ground. Moon Watcher squatted and watched. Wolf thought he saw traces of a smile on the warrior's face. He could not help but like this guy, even though the Apache might have a knife ripping open Wolf's throat ten minutes from now.

Wolf began stacking the coins, all double eagles, on the ground in groups of five. "One hundred dollars in each stack," he said.

Jael repeated in Apache, and Moon Watcher nodded.

Suddenly, the proceedings were interrupted by the frantic yelling of a breathless young warrior racing toward the trading group. He came up to El Gato and began speaking rapidly to the chief and pointing southward. Wolf could not understand a word, but he had a sick feeling that the party was beginning. He continued counting out the gold coins, although Moon Watcher's head was turned toward the excited conversation. El Gato looked at Jael, his face purple with rage, and screamed at her for several minutes, before sprinting away with One Hand and four of the spectator warriors. Wolf saw the two warriors that remained with Moon Watcher raise their rifles.

"What is going on?" Wolf asked Jael.

"Two guards in the south canyon have disappeared. Their relief guards cannot find them. Also, one of One Hand's wives says that Sunrise is missing. I think Sunrise is his third wife. El Gato doesn't know the worst of it yet. And we are not to leave until El Gato returns."

"To hell with that." Wolf's hand moved to his Colt and slipped it from the holster. He got to his feet poised to fire at the two warriors holding rifles waist high and pointed at Wolf's midsection.

Moon Watcher spoke, his words crisp and authoritative. To Wolf's astonishment, the warriors lowered their rifles.

"He essentially told them to stand down," Jael said.

Moon Watcher spoke again to Jael, and she nodded her head.

She turned to Wolf. "He says we should go. He can do nothing more for us. He cannot count money anyway. He asked if it was true that I spoke for the tribes, and I explained that I am a lawyer and that is what I do. He asked if I would speak for his band if they returned to the reservation, and I said I would. Damn, I don't have any business cards with me. I'll have to figure out how to get in touch. I think I picked up a new client. Maybe I can charge my time to the firm as a business trip."

"The only business I'm interested in is getting out of this place." Leaving the gold and saddlebags on the ground, Wolf moved for his stallion, and Jael was only a step behind.

Wolf took the lead, followed by the captives mounted on their two horses, the girls Wolf thought of as the

Feather sisters, sharing the mount just behind him. The smaller of the twins clung to the taller one's waist like a wood tick and gritted her teeth and sealed her eyes when she got her first look at the seemingly bottomless canyon below. Jael, astride her bay, lagged as a rear guard.

Wolf relaxed just a bit after they left the mesa behind and got a good start down the winding trail. Then the sound of three distinct shots from above echoed through the mountains. A signal? They would learn soon enough.

Chapter 28

TABITHA DEPARTED HER wickiup with water containers suspended from a slender pole perched behind her neck and slung across her shoulders. She was angling toward the southern segment of the stream when she heard the commotion at the north end of the village. Oliver had arrived she assumed. She hoped Sunrise did not encounter delays. They must move quickly, although the destination was rather vague.

How could they connect with Cal and Delgado in the wilderness they would encounter below the mesa? Jael had assured her they need not search. They would be found. She guessed she had no choice. Trust, she reminded herself. When she reached the stream where the water dropped a few feet over its rocky bed, their agreed meeting place, she lifted the water jugs from her shoulders and dropped them on the ground.

She did not see Sunrise. She thought she felt her heart skip a bit or two. What if Sunrise did not show up? Then the petite Navajo woman stepped from behind a curtain of pines on the other side of the stream and ran toward her, splashing through the water that nearly swallowed her legs as she fought the current. Tabitha extended a hand from the bank's edge, and Sunrise grasped it, holding tight as Tabitha pulled her up to the bank.

"I come too soon," Sunrise said. "Afraid I not be here when you come."

Now, a decision must be made. She knew there were two trails down the canyon, one on each side of the stream. But there would be guards, and her chances of getting near enough during daylight to use her knife were close to nil. She decided to head for the narrow trail on the west side of the stream. Pursuers would be unlikely to move horses down the canyon there. Of course, they would be easy targets for bows and rifles on the opposite side. She wondered if they would die this day.

She turned in the direction of the village to confirm that no one had sighted them. Again, her heart raced when she saw someone running their way. A skirt flapped in the wind. A woman. Walks Far bearing a message? No. It couldn't be. Cactus Bloom. She clutched the hilt of her knife. She did not like the woman, but she had no desire to kill her. It would be terrible to render Cactus Bloom's children motherless. But she was prepared to take the woman's life if she had no other option.

"Stand behind me," Tabitha instructed Sunrise.

Cactus Bloom stopped when she was within five paces. For the first time, Tabitha saw no hate in the woman's eyes. Tabitha had picked up only a smattering of Apache during her stay in the village, but she understood the word for "white man" when El Gato's senior wife repeated it and pointed toward forested high ground a good hundred yards beyond the west side of the stream near the base of the mountain that stretched above the mesa. A trap?

Again, in Apache, Cactus Bloom said, "Go."

Tabitha made a snap decision. She nodded at her former nemesis, whirled, grabbed Sunrise's hand and nearly drug her along as she ran for the stream. She helped the smaller woman struggle against the water's force as they crossed. They collapsed on the bank when they emerged from the water, catching their breaths for a few moments. Tabitha saw that Cactus Bloom still stood across the stream. Again, she pointed toward the wooded high ground. Then she turned away and hurried back toward the village.

"We must go," she told Sunrise, still not knowing what to make of Cactus Bloom's directions. She thought the woman hated her, but why would she help her? Of course, Tabitha's escape from the village would eliminate the object of the senior wife's jealously. That would be a pragmatic reason. But somehow, Tabitha sensed it was more than that. How many times had she heard the words of her rancher father? "More often than not, things just ain't what they seem. Look a little harder if you're trying to get at the truth."

Tabitha and Sunrise got up, picked up their small bags and started running for the high ground in the direction Cactus Bloom had pointed. They put yards behind them quickly on the flat but slowed as the ground began to slope. As the incline steepened, Tabitha worried that she would be forced to stop and wait for the Navajo woman, but Sunrise gamely kept pace until they gained the high ground and disappeared into the trees. Hidden from any pursuers' sight for the moment, they dropped to the ground, each finding a pine to lean her back against.

"We cannot rest long here. We must keep moving. Someone will learn we are missing if Cactus Bloom hasn't told them already—and if this isn't a trap she set."

"No trap, Little Sis."

Tabitha started and tossed a look over her shoulder. Her eyes widened in disbelief. "Cal, I don't believe it." She stood up and fell into her brother's outstretched arms. Delgado had stepped out from the trees and already helped Sunrise to her feet, holding her firmly while she sobbed uncontrollably.

Tabitha pulled away from Cal and looked up at her brother, wiping silent tears from her eyes with the backs of her hands.

"I didn't know how we would find you. I thought you were somewhere near the bottom of the canyon. I didn't even make the connection when Cactus Bloom said 'white man' and pointed this way. She wasn't making any sense to me, but she was insistent we come here."

"Who's Cactus Bloom?"

"El Gato's wife. She's my boss, so to speak. I'm his second wife . . . or was."

"You married that son-of-a-bitch?"

"Not exactly. I was a wife by claim or declaration, I guess."

"I don't want to hear any more about it," Cal snapped.

He obviously was uncomfortable with the implications of her being El Gato's wife. Wait until he heard the whole story. She would spare him for now.

"But how would Cactus Bloom know you were up here?"

"I don't know, unless she saw me last night."

"I don't understand."

"I sneaked in last night to scout out the place, maybe see if I could find you. A woman was standing outside a lodge with her arms folded across her chest. She looked my way, but I thought I ducked behind one of the lodges in time. She didn't scream or nothing. When I peeked out a few minutes later, I couldn't see hide nor hair of her. I beat the hell out of there. I suppose she could have followed me and seen where I went."

Tabitha guessed El Gato would have been with her at the time. She shuddered at the thought the woman waited at night for her husband's return or, worse yet, spied outside Tabitha's wickiup. It still didn't explain why Cactus Bloom did not alert El Gato, unless she suspected someone was coming for Tabitha or was going to wait and see. Tabitha's rescue would not have disappointed Cactus Bloom. She supposed she would never know for certain why or how the good turn came about.

She glanced at Delgado and Sunrise. They were speaking softly, and Tabitha guessed Sunrise would be explaining about the ransom of Fears Nothing.

"So how do we get out of this place?" Tabitha asked.

"Swim."

"Swim?"

"That so-called stream is a baby river. It moves fast and is deep enough to carry us to the mouth of the canyon. It's been tested. Take my word for it. We'll have some bruises, but we can win a race out of the canyon."

Tabitha could swim like an otter, and she knew Cal was more than a passable swimmer. They had skinny dipped in mountain lakes on the Rivers Slash R as children until, for reasons she had not understood until years later, Cal had suddenly turned shy and would not swim unless he wore his undershorts. But swimming would not be required in this stream. The water would do the work if the swimmers could handle the punishment from the rocks.

"When do we go?"

"Wait a minute." Cal stepped away, walked over to the tree line and looked out over the village in the distance. "Now. There's a bunch headed for the canyon. They must have finally figured out their lookouts took a vacation to Mexico City. We'd better beat the hell out of here. Bring your things and follow me."

Cal hurried southerly, soon leaving the woods behind and moving into the rocks, pressing everyone to keep pace with his long strides. He came to a huge cleavage in the rock wall overlooking the canyon, splitting the wall like a giant axe had been driven into the stone. Rifle and possible bag in his hands, Cal plumped down on his buttocks, pushed his legs into the crevice, pushed off and disappeared. "Next," he hollered.

All Tabitha could see was a black hole, but she followed her brother's example, flinching as the shale and small stones stabbed her backside as she slid down a chute-like slope into Cal's arms. Sunrise came next, followed by Delgado.

"Keep moving," Cal said, as he started walking down a gentle slope that led away from the entryway.

Tabitha felt like they were confined in a tunnel, but a sliver of light overhead that widened as they moved ahead allowed her to see Cal in front of her, and, for the first time, she noticed he seemed to be leaning some to his right, forearm pressed against his side. "Cal, are you hurt?" she asked.

"I'm fine," he growled. His tone said he was not going to talk about it.

Abruptly, they came around a curve in the crevice, and the sun's glare through the opening blinded her for an instant. They paused, and she could hear the rush of the stream splashing over the rocks on its journey to the canyon floor. Cal raised his hand to signal a stop. He stepped forward and peered out the opening, then backed away.

"I hear them upstream," he said, "coming this way. There's a lone Apache keeping watch from the trail on the other side downstream a ways. I got to take him out. When my rifle cracks, head out of here and make tracks down the bank. Hit the water. Try to float on your backs. Maybe you can hold your stuff to your bellies and try to keep it dry but don't count on it." He hesitated, "Girls, those skirts ain't going to help none. They get wet, and they'll drag you down."

He didn't need to say more. Tabitha removed her moccasins and added them to the contents of her possible bag. Both women began to strip away their bulky Mexican-style skirts, oblivious to their lack of undergarments. Tabitha left her skirt where it fell, thinking she would welcome the change to her buckskin britches if she got out of the stream alive. If not, what did it matter? Sunrise stuffed her skirt into her bag.

As soon as they were ready, Cal slipped out onto the trail, and Delgado edged up behind him with his own rifle. Tabitha heard two shots and sprinted out the opening, leaped over the trail's edge and slid down the rugged slope of the stream's bank. When her feet hit the water, she regained her footing for a moment, then, clutching her bag to her chest, lay back in the water and let it carry her away.

She caught a brief glimpse of the dead Apache warrior sprawled on the east bank as she swept by and wished she could stop and grab his rifle, but she was long past him by the time she completed the thought. The stream was like a ride on a bucking bronco, tossing the body randomly and setting it down hard. She knew because she had ridden a few on the Slash R. Twice the turbulent waters spat her out, once slamming her hip against a protruding boulder, another time propelling her shoulder against a tree stump at water's edge. Her bag was soaked by now, but she held fast to it.

Once she looked back over her shoulder to confirm that her companions followed. Sunrise was not far behind and appeared to be almost skimming the water. Her weight likely did not reach much more than a hundred pounds and likely was an advantage here. Cal rode the roiling stream far behind the others. She figured his massive body would make well over two of Sunrise and was likely taking a hammering.

She saw that the canyon narrowed noticeably ahead, and the stream seemed to narrow and deepen suddenly. Without more warning, she struck the rapids, and this time the bucking bronco did not throw her but gave her the ride of a lifetime before she shot over a small fall and the canyon widened and the water spread with it and leveled off. This had to be the mouth Cal was talking about. She paddled toward the west side until her hand touched the streambed. She rolled over and clambered to her feet, her eyes immediately searching for her companions. She saw Sunrise coming and walked back into the water until it was knee-high, reaching out and grabbing the Navajo woman's hand before she swept by, helping her back to the shallows where she could gain footing. Delgado was not far back, rifle and cartridge bag held high above his head, but still riding the rapids. Cal was not in sight.

She saw that Sunrise was pulling on her sopping skirt and it reminded her of her own half-nakedness. She dug into her bag, tugging out her wet buckskins as she made her way to some brush beyond the stream's bed. She stripped off the saturated peasant's blouse, squeezed the worst of the water from the garment and stuffed it in the bag. Then she worked the wet, resisting buckskin shirt over her head and shoulders. After another struggle with britches and moccasins, she was clothed again but had gained no warmth. The brilliant sun and dry mountain air would resolve that problem soon enough she thought.

Delgado had made it to the bank and was standing there, his eyes fixed upstream and one arm wrapped about his wife's shoulders. Cal had still not arrived. Now she was worried. He had been trailing behind the others, but not tremendously far back. He should have arrived by now. Gunfire. First, a single shot echoed through the canyon, then a flurry. More than one shooter. The Apaches must have caught up with Cal.

If any of the shots came from Cal, he would not be in the water. She wondered if his rifle would have taken in too much water to fire. She had seen him wrap his Peacemaker in deerskin and slip it into his possible bag with cartridges for both firearms. Nothing in her bag had remained dry. She waited. More gunshots. She watched the rapids, half expecting her brother's bullet-riddled body to come tumbling over the waterfall.

Delgado turned her way and said, "He told me we should not wait for him. We are to circle the mountain and follow the gap that Cal and I took to get to here, then on to our meeting place to connect with the others." The thought of leaving Cal behind horrified Tabitha, but she had no weapon besides her knife. Delgado headed for the woods with Sunrise a step behind him. She hesitated and looked upstream once more, then turned away and followed her friends.

Chapter 29

UPON BEING TOLD about the missing guards, El Gato had ordered all but two of the warriors to follow him, directing them to alert all the village warriors to possible attack. One Hand split off to check on the whereabouts of his wife, Sunrise. The traders had attempted to ransom the Navajo woman, and it made El Gato suspicious that the visitors were not the persons he had thought them to be. At least they did not know about Ta-Bee. Or did they? He ordered the warriors to the south canyon and hurried to Ta-Bee's wickiup. He did not see her in the vicinity, so he peered inside. He could discern no changes.

El Gato then rushed to the lodge he shared with Cactus Bloom. Nothing appeared out of the ordinary. The children played nearby, and his wife was stretching skins on a rack. He stepped up to her. "Have you seen Ta-Bee?" he demanded.

She turned and met his glare with dark, defiant eyes. "Ta-Bee? I think she collects water from the stream."

"You are supposed to watch her."

"Why? She is not my child."

Her increasing insolence was angering him. She had never feared him like a proper Apache wife should. He raised his fist to strike, and she just stared at him, almost daring him to hit her. He lowered his fist and raced away, heading for the stream and collecting another dozen warriors along the way. When he arrived at the stream, he sprinted along the bank looking for his second wife. Then he came upon the empty water jars scattered on the ground. This confirmed his fears, and rage overtook him.

El Gato ordered one of the warriors to gather others to assure the traders were restrained from departing with the captives. "Give the signal to those guarding the north passage," he said.

He realized now that he would never hold Ta-Bee. He could never trust her. She was a warrior woman, and his life was in danger every night he lay with her. He had been a fool. He would track her down and catch her, but he would not bring her back. He would kill her, and the black, soaring scavengers in the sky would dispose of her remains.

He was still perplexed, however. She would not have had time to kill the guards, although he did not doubt the conniving witch's ability to do so. Others had to be involved. But how many? His scouts would have picked up a large party. Certainly, they would have not overlooked anyone on horseback.

One Hand joined him now. "Sunrise has left the village," the older warrior said.

"She must be with Ta-Bee. Take the warriors and find them. They must be on one of the canyon trails. Do what you will with Sunrise but hold Ta-Bee for me. I will deal with her."

He decided to return to the traders. They were involved in this. He was certain of it. As he hurried back to the exchange site, he heard three rifle shots signaling the closing of the north trail. This White Wolf and She Who Speaks had much to answer for.

When he arrived at the lonely pine tree, he found that the traders and ransomed captives had disappeared. Moon Watcher and the two warriors at his side stood there as if waiting for his return. When he approached, Moon Watcher extended the gold-filled saddlebags. "The ransom," his old comrade said.

El Gato accepted the bags, searching Moon Watcher's eyes for an explanation but received none. "The traders and the captives. Where are they? I told you to hold them."

"I am done with this. I do not wish a life of war for my children. The white soldiers are too many. We kill one and two replace him. Reservation life cannot be worse than what we soon will face here. I am taking my family back to San Carlos. There are others who will go with me."

El Gato's first instinct was to take his knife and kill Moon Watcher for his betrayal, but the man carried no weapon, and all could see that. Also, the two warriors who stood beside his former friend appeared to be Moon Watcher loyalists. He said, "We will talk of this later," and turned and walked away. He would secure the gold at his wickiup, and then he must track down Ta-Bee and recover the captives. Many would pay for what had happened this day.

Chapter 30

THE APACHE WARRIOR posted on the first rock outcropping already had his rifle aimed at Wolf's chest when the descending party approached. He said something in Apache, which Wolf assumed was an order to stop and a threat to kill. A rifle shot cracked and a blot of scarlet erupted on the Apache's naked chest before he stumbled backward and toppled over the escarpment's edge, dropping like a slain bird on his way to the cliff's bottom.

Wolf looked back up the trail and waved thanks to Jael, who held her rifle high in acknowledgment, and then nudged Owl ahead. He heard a smattering of gunfire from below and knew that North Star and Fears Nothing were now engaged with the hostiles. He worried that one man and a small boy could not hold out for long. Wolf's riders had to get past another Apache sentry before shaking free to help. Their position on the trail provided a decided advantage in picking up targets, but their rock cover was meager, and they would not be able to advance downslope without exposing themselves. The trail was not a strategic place to be under siege with both ends plugged.

The gunshots ceased for a time. Wolf hoped it meant they had reached a stand-off and that North Star and the boy had not been overrun. They came to a sharp turn in the trail, and it warned him the other lookout was posted around the bend. Jael could not offer cover this time. He dismounted and slipped his old Army Colt from its holster. Owl would stand in place till whistled forward. He backed up against the stone mountain wall, inching step by step around the bend in the trail. When the path started to straighten, he stepped out, swinging his pistol in the direction where the guard had been posted. The move had been unnecessary. The guard was stretched out face-down on the trail, apparently dead. Wolf approached and knelt, rolling the Apache over on his back and pushing the corpse off the trail. Gaping holes in the warrior's head and neck. Rifle gone, possibly over the trail's edge.

He whistled for Owl, and the horse walked around the turn, the others of their party following. Rifles cracked down the trail again, diverting attention from his confused thoughts. He mounted the stallion and winced when he heard shots from behind. Apaches from the village. Jael was on her own. There was no way he could make a turn and get past the other horses on the trail. He reined Owl forward, picking up the pace as much as he dared. A misstep would carry horse and rider to death.

As Jael and her bay cleared the turn, Wolf looked back and was relieved to find she appeared unharmed. The same probably could not be said for one or two of the Apaches following her.

When she closed the gap with the other riders, Jael yelled at Wolf, "I took down two, but there are more coming, and they're closing." She turned in the saddle, raised the Winchester to her shoulder and fired two more shots. "Just keep moving, I'll try to slow them down."

Finally, Wolf could see North Star and Fears Nothing dug in on the trail ahead. Two dead Apaches lay beyond them. As he rode up, he noticed that an extra rifle lay beside Fears Nothing. He looked at North Star. "You got the Apache guard?"

"Fears Nothing did. I stayed here. The boy insisted one of us should be further up the trail in case there was trouble up that way."

Wolf looked at the boy, who lay belly-down with his Winchester pointed down the trail.

North Star pointed down the trail. "One of those is his, too."

Wolf shook his head in disbelief. "Well, we've got company coming from up the hill, and we've got to break through."

North Star said, "It looks like the other three have started up the trail now. We're going to get pinched between."

"North Star, why don't you go help Jael fight off the bunch coming down from the mesa. Fears Nothing, you can follow me. Stay about ten paces back. Take down anybody that gets past me."

Wolf whipped out the Colt again and reined the stallion down the trail toward the oncoming Apaches. He hated to expose his treasured Owl this way, but the trail had to be cleared if there was to be any chance for escape. As they moved steadily toward the warriors, a rifle cracked, and shards of rock splintered off a protruding stone above his head. He fired two shots at the attackers, knowing he was short of the Colt's effective range yet, but he got the warriors' attention. They froze in place momentarily, seemingly in disbelief that he was riding directly at them. The front Apache then raised his rifle and squeezed off another round, missing wildly. This time, Wolf holstered the Colt and pulled the Winchester from its scabbard.

The Apache got off another shot, and the stallion shrieked and stumbled forward before righting himself and continuing his pace down the trail. Wolf shook off the reality that if Owl went down, he probably joined his horse in the chasm off the mountainside. He squeezed his legs tightly to the stallion's sides to balance himself and wrapped the reins around the saddle horn. He levered a cartridge into the chamber of the rifle, raised it, and squeezed the trigger. Owl did not even flinch at the gun's explosion and continued toward the Apaches, who were one less now. The downed warriors turned and began to run down the trail to the mountain's base. Wolf dismounted to examine his horse, but Fears Nothing whipped past him, giving chase to the fleeing Apaches.

"Let them go," Wolf yelled at the Navajo boy.

Fears Nothing either did not hear or chose not to. The boy moved like lightning and was closing the gap on the stocky, slower warrior, leaping over the body of the Apache Wolf had killed and continuing the race, until he stopped, knelt, raised his rifle and fired two quick shots, launching his target off the mountainside. Wolf relaxed when the boy sat down on the trail, apparently catching his breath. He seemed satisfied with his harvest for the moment.

Wolf saw that Jael and the others were moving his way, North Star walking behind and keeping an eye out for the Apaches behind them. He anticipated that the enemy had concluded that a battle on the mountainside was futile unless the trail was blocked at its outlet. He was certain, however, that the Apaches were far from abandoning pursuit.

He searched Owl for the wound that had caused him to briefly falter, his fingers tracing up the stallion's chest and upper legs. He found the wound in the horse's thickly muscled shoulder, barely visible and only light bleeding where the slug had burrowed. He probed the edges of the wound and thought he felt the swelling where the lead was imbedded. If true, that meant the bullet could likely be extracted without serious damage. He could do the job if he had to, but North Star was the best horseman he had ever encountered, and Wolf figured he would recruit his new friend's help.

He took Owl's reins and started leading him down the trail. He stopped along the way to push the Apache's body to the trail's edge and then continued the trek to meet up with Fears Nothing, who stood waiting with rifle in hand. When Wolf reached him, the boy was grinning broadly. "Told you I could shoot," he said.

Wolf smiled back. "You did. And I doubted you. I apologize. You did good work today."

The boy held up the rifle. "This was the Apache's rifle. Mine now?"

Wolf noted that it was a relatively new Winchester, likely taken off some dead rancher or homesteader or purchased from a Comanchero-like trader. "I'd say so."

"I will kill some more Apaches."

The boy was liking this too much for Wolf's comfort. He had never taken pleasure in killing any man and had hoped he was finished with this sort of thing. "I hope the killing's about over," he said, fearing that they were far from done.

When they reached the base of the mountain, Wolf did not see any sign of the surviving Apache. Since all the Apache horses had disappeared, he assumed he had taken off with the horses. He was relieved to find that their horses and mule were still where they had been tied in the trees. Runs Alone, the young Navajo woman, informed him she could handle a rifle, not expertly but with some competence. He gave her the old Winchester Fears Nothing had used before claiming the dead Apache's newer weapon.

While the two women and Fears Nothing kept the Apaches pinned down on the mountain ledge and backed the riders up beyond range, Wolf had North Star examine Owl's bullet wound. The horseman scrutinized it and tested the surrounding flesh with his fingers. "You're right," he said, "the slug's buried just under the skin. Pull his head away and hold tight."

Wolf pulled the reins tight and wrapped his arm as far as it would go about the stallion's neck. He watched as North Star took the point of his skinning knife, made a small slice over the entry wound and squeezed. A bloody chunk of lead popped out, followed by a rivulet of blood. Owl had reacted with only token resistance, not even challenging the limits of Wolf's powerful arms.

"Let it drain," North Star suggested. "We'll fix a poultice to apply when we get settled in someplace. Maybe you can ride that big gelding of Cal's for now and give your stallion a break. A day's rest, and I think he will be ready to ride."

The gunfire had ceased, and Wolf returned to Jael and the other two defenders. He looked toward the mountain and saw a line of mounted warriors, at least a dozen, lined up single file over a hundred yards up the trail.

"They're waiting us out," Jael said. "Perfect targets if they come any farther, but they know we can't wait here long. They've got war parties out that will hit us sooner or later."

"Then we need to get back to the rendezvous site and fort up."

Chapter 31

TABITHA HEARD GUNFIRE from the north and noticed the worried eyes of Delgado and Sunrise as they turned their heads in that direction. She understood. The fate of their son, Fears Nothing, would depend upon the fortunes of Wolf's rescue party. Gunfire was rarely good news. And there was still no sign of Cal.

From the position of the afternoon sun, it appeared they were headed northwest, walking crossways along a slope on narrow trails fit only for deer and goats, she thought. By Tabitha's calculation they must be on the other side of the mountain that rose up and cast a shadow over the mesa where the Apache stronghold was located. Delgado had traveled the route before, so they were not delayed by decision-making. He knew where they were headed and how to get there. But could they outrun the Apaches, at least to a place where they might make a stand?

Her buckskins had dried, and she savored the sun's rays that bathed her back with warmth. They walked briskly along the path that crisscrossed with many others, and, occasionally, Delgado would alter course and move onto one of the pathways that dovetailed into the current route. Earlier, they had heard the chattering of Apache voices some distance behind them. The hunters had quickly surmised the direction the prey had gone. Delgado had explained that the exit to the east was nearly impassable and hiking deeper into Mexico would have made no sense, so brilliant deduction was not required by the Apaches to guess their course. They likely had left tracks and other sign near the stream.

What bothered her most was that she no longer heard Apache voices. There was no way the Apaches would have abandoned the search. El Gato would never quit until he reclaimed or killed her, more likely the latter. If only she had a rifle. Her Henry with ammunition would be best, but she would settle for anything that responded to a trigger squeeze. They had a single rifle among them and could not be certain it had not been rendered impotent by the water-drenching it had taken earlier. She hoped the weapon had been revived by the dry air and radiant sun. She knew that Delgado had spent time wiping the gun down and trying to clean it with a long reed.

Suddenly, an Apache warrior emerged from the trees on the slope above them, his rifle leveled at Delgado. Then another with bowstring nocked with an arrow pulled taut appeared in front of them. Her worries had been well founded. The warrior facing Delgado screamed at him, but, of course, they could not understand. A gunshot rang out, and the Apache with the bow toppled backward with blood flowing from his temple, the arrow from his bowstring's release driving into the dirt. Another shot took down the second warrior who rolled down the slope and came to rest not more than five feet from Tabitha.

She looked upward in the direction of the gunfire, seeing nothing until Cal stepped from behind a tree and started down the slope, struggling to maintain his balance on the shifting shale. "Guess the gun still works," he said.

Then she saw that the right side of his shirt was blood-soaked. "Cal, what happened?"

"Opened up an old war wound, I guess. Some feller tried carving up my ribs on my trip to visit my little sis. Ain't bad, but our swim got it bleeding again." He called to Delgado, "Hey, Delgado. Need another patch job."

Tabitha plucked her nearly dry blouse from her bag and gave it to Delgado, who had already started cutting strips from the bottom of Sunrise's skirt for bandages. He helped himself to a few more scraps from the blouse and quickly went to work rebinding Cal's rib wound. "It cannot heal unless you rest, but I see no sickness in the flesh."

"Well, we ain't going to be resting for a spell. Let me catch my wind a few minutes, then we'd best be on our way."

Tabitha asked, "What happened? Where were you?"

"Got hung up on some rocks, and the devils was coming down the trail like a pack of wolves. I climbed out on the other side. Prayed the rifle would work and gave 'em some lead to ponder. Took out at least one and slowed them some. Then I got up and beat the hell down trail. Move like a racehorse when I'm scared. You was gone like you should've been, and I took a high trail, so I wouldn't lead them right to you. Saw them varmints headed your way below me, though, so I followed."

"But there are others chasing us?"

"Yep. But no more than a half dozen, I'd guess. It's slower than a turtle's pace bringing a horse through this way, so they're afoot like us. I'm betting the others headed back to go down the north trail to catch us when we hit American territory."

"El Gato won't quit, wherever he is," Tabitha said. She walked over and picked up the dead Apache's rifle. "At least we've got another gun." The feel of the weapon in her hands increased her confidence immeasurably. She knelt and worked an Army cartridge belt over the Apache's shoulder and tugged it away from the corpse. Then she ducked her head through it and pulled the belt over her own shoulder as she stood up. She had given El Gato a pass her first opportunity to kill him. Fatherhood would grant "the cat" no immunity if they met up again.

Cal slipped into the woods to watch the perimeters as Delgado took up the lead again, and the party continued the winding path northward.

Chapter 32

WOLF LED THE captives toward the rendezvous site, pushing the horses at a breakneck pace. Jael and North Star had taken up positions as outriders some thirty feet distant on each side of the column, and reluctantly Wolf had given in to Fears Nothing's plea to act as rear guard. Eight or so Apache warriors had caught up with the fleeing riders, splitting off and riding parallel to Wolf's party, firing rifles intermittently and loosing occasional arrows that fell far short and died in the dust. So far, the outriders were holding them at bay, and Jael's marksmanship had dropped one of the attackers, warning the Apaches to keep their distance.

Wolf was certain a larger party was forming somewhere not far behind the others, probably led by El Gato. He had sensed the dissension in the village and wondered if some of the band might decline to join the pursuit. There was no way of knowing. It was late afternoon but still several hours from sunset when he caught sight of the rise and trees near the spring where their search party had split up a few days earlier. It would have been impossible for Cal and Delgado, hopefully accompanied by Tabby and Sunrise, to have arrived yet. They might be forced to hold out here for a day or more, and if the escape at the south outlet from the Apache stronghold had turned sour, he couldn't try to pull out for several more days. He would not depart without his friends until he had judged prospects of their return hopeless.

Rifles cracked several times off to Wolf's left and a quick glance confirmed North Star had left another Apache mount riderless, causing the attackers to pull back some more. Wolf's experience during the Comanche wars had convinced him there were only a few marksmen among the Indian nations. Rifles were yet new additions to their weapons of warfare, as complex for them to refine and master the skill to fire accurately as for white foes to grasp the techniques demanded of the bow and arrow. Attempting to use the weapon effectively from horseback would be even more challenging.

Wolf was confident his party could fight off this small band easily enough, but if others showed up in serious numbers the outcome was far from certain. As they reached the woods, he dismounted, and while Jael and North Star held off the Apaches, who appeared to be pulling back now, he helped Runs Alone and the Feather twins from their horses. Runs Alone immediately took her rifle and joined Fears Nothing in providing cover for Jael and North Star as the two outriders now reined their mounts in a race toward the cover of the trees.

When they were all sheltered in the wooded area near the spring, Wolf considered how best to utilize his few defenders. They could not allow the Apaches to get to the horses. Without the mounts any attempt to escape from the place would be futile. The sparse grass here had already been grazed down from the first visit, but there were remnants for a day. He decided that the horses should be staked out on a short tether and their defense set up around the animals. He did not like the idea of putting the horses within the range of fire, but the risk of losing the entire remuda to Apache stealth and theft outweighed the risk. The trees would offer at least some protection.

After staking out the horses within an irregular ring of dispersed rifle stations, Wolf and his companions dragged dead wood and rolled nearby stones to the defensive spots to offer a smattering of cover for the shooters. When that was finished, he spoke with Jael and North Star about a thought that had been nagging him.

"I keep thinking that if I had horses waiting when Cal and the others break free from the mountain slopes, we could cut hours off their travel time. They would reinforce our position here until we could organize to make a run for it—if that looked like the best option."

"Could you find the place?" Jael asked.

"I'm sure I could get in the vicinity. Delgado said they would be coming over the backside of the mountain that rises above the west edge of the Apache stronghold. They are passing through a vee where two mountain ridges connect. They will likely head to the low end of the trough when they break into the foothills."

"The sun's about burnt out. Can you find it in the dark?"

"Moonlight would be enough. I'd take Cal's and Delgado's horses with me, and the darkness would help me slip by with them. But can you hold off the Apaches with four guns?"

"We have the ammunition. It just depends on numbers. From listening to Tabby and her friend, Walks Far, I think there is a good chance some warriors in the village will sit this dance out. Anyway, they won't make a run until more show up, and it's a good bet they wouldn't do anything before sunrise."

"You can't count on that."

"No. But they won't catch us by surprise, so any advantage of night attack washes out. I think you should try to find Tabby and the others."

"I will. But I'll turn back in time to be here by daybreak if they don't show up."

Chapter 33

As the sun disappeared over the west mountain ridge, Tabitha felt uneasy. The others seemed to welcome the night and the ebbing of heat. Cal, blond and fair-complexioned, had never thrived that well under baking sun rays and appeared to be dragging some. The periodic seeping of blood from his rib wound was likely taking a toll as well. She, however, derived no comfort from the onset of darkness. Twice El Gato had found her in the night, taking her captive on the second occasion. Her life with him had largely been confined to the hours after sundown. In her mind, El Gato was a creature of the night, forever stalking, lurking, waiting for the right moment.

Tabitha did not buy in to the notion that El Gato had returned to the village to join in the chase of Jael, Wolf and the others down the north trail. She was his obsession, and she had betrayed him. His anger went beyond any bruise to his ego. There was a slim chance he might recapture her and hold her until the child was born. But she had no illusions. Whether this night or later, in El Gato's mind, she had earned a death sentence. While this man lived, the nights would always portend danger, not only for her but for her unborn child.

They paused to rest, not bothering to sit down, simply bending over to catch a breath or lean against a tree. Cal said, "I'm thinking two hours to the foothills at our present pace."

"At least that," Delgado said. "Another three or four after that to the meet-up place. But I don't like it."

"Don't like what?"

"Anything. It's too quiet for one thing. Either we lost them, or they know where we're at and are biding their time for the right moment."

"You sure as hell know how to cheer a feller up, but I ain't arguing against what you say. But I don't know what we do except go on and keep an eye out."

Tabitha said, "Let's be honest. Sooner or later, they will run us down. This is how they live. Apache warriors can run for days if they have to." She could not fault Cal, but he was about done in from all he had been through.

She and Sunrise were hanging tough, but they were not conditioned as warriors. And Delgado was a farmer.

Cal said, "You're right, Little Sis. I don't want to fight those devils in the woods if I can help it. If we can make it to the foothills, I'd say we find a likely spot and set up and wait a spell. Take 'em on where we can see them."

They will not wait until we reach the foothills, Tabitha thought. El Gato is with them, and he will want to pounce in the darkness of the forest. He was out there. She could almost feel his hot breath upon her neck, his claws digging into her breasts. She pushed away from the tree where she had been resting and headed up the trail at a trot. The others fell in quickly behind her.

She did not keep up that pace for long, but she felt better. Somehow, it was life affirming that she could still move, enabling her to shake off the pessimism that had struck her earlier. The others caught up with her soon, and she felt Delgado slip past her to take the lead again. Nearly an hour later he came to a barely discernable path that forked off their present trail and angled down the mountain slope.

"We are making progress," Delgado said. "The forest will start to thin soon—and then the foothills."

Ten minutes later, a rifle's blast echoed through the mountains, and Delgado groaned. He crumpled to his knees, dropped his Winchester and tumbled off the trail and into some brambly brush. Sunrise rushed to his side, tugging him away from the brush, while Cal and Tabitha returned futile shots at what might as well have been a ghost.

Tabitha said, “Cal, keep an eye out. Let me take a look at Delgado.”

“Not about to take a nap, Little Sis.” He backed up to the charred trunk of a lightning-struck pine.

She knelt beside Sunrise and helped her pull Delgado nearer to Cal’s position. This was not a time to spread out, whatever vulnerability they might have bunched up. Delgado was conscious and seemed to be recovering from the initial shock. At first, she feared her friend had been gut-shot, but Sunrise had lifted his shirt and pulled his britches down a bit, and it appeared the bullet had struck him high in the hip. She had taken his knife and was again sacrificing more of her skirt to bandages. Soon the obviously adept woman was staunching the bleeding and appeared to have the immediate treatment under control, allowing Tabitha to move back to Cal.

“Any thoughts?” she asked her brother.

“Duck.”

They both dropped as a rifle fired from behind a tree upslope, showing the briefest flash of light before a bullet chipped off a chunk of tree stump. Cal's Winchester replied twice, and a shadowy figure pitched forward, and a rifle clattered on the rocks.

"There's more up that way," Cal said as he crawled back up the trail.

Tabitha did not like his slipping away but knew their cause was hopeless if they did not somehow take the fight to their enemy. She cast a glance at Delgado. He was on the ground, back pressed against the stump, but his rifle was now cradled in his arms. Sunrise knelt beside him, knife clutched in her hand. Good. There was no running now. They had to make their stand here. One more gun improved their odds just a bit and freed her to move away from the cluster that made it too easy for the attackers' weapons to hit a target.

She got to her feet and took a few steps in the direction Cal had gone, thinking she might back him, but her brother had disappeared into the trees. For the moment, gunfire had ceased, and she assumed Cal was stalking Apaches. She wondered if they were also stalking him. Suddenly, an arm clamped around her neck, cutting off her air and yanking her backwards. She was vaguely aware of the rifle slipping from her hands as she was dragged off into the woods, and she could barely hear

Sunrise's faint voice calling her name in the distance before blackness carried her away.

WHEN SHE AWAKENED, Tabby was not surprised to see El Gato standing above her. Smiling. Not good. He almost never smiled. She realized then she was naked and reflexively raised her arms to cover herself but discovered neither arms nor legs would move. He had anchored wrists and ankles to nearby saplings. He had apparently dragged her some distance.

El Gato moved over her, standing with legs straddling her body. He brandished a knife, one she recognized—the one she had stolen. "Kill baby. No good. Ta-Bee see." He pantomimed his plan, drawing the knife in the air above her belly and stomping on the ground.

Oh, God. He was going to slice her open and tear the fetus out while she was alive. And then stomp her child into the earth while she watched and died. She had known fear on this journey and others she had made, but never such total terror. It hurt to give him the satisfaction, but she screamed. And screamed, only vaguely aware of the gunshots and battle being waged in the distance.

El Gato lowered himself to his knees, his naked thighs brushing her hips. The hardness pushing against his breechclout and pressing her flesh revealed his excitement as the knife tip inched toward her. She was screamed out now and silent. She closed her eyes so tightly they hurt as she awaited the blade.

Then she felt him fall away and someone was rolling on the ground with El Gato. A bigger man. Cal? All she could see were shadows. El Gato bounced up, swinging his knife viciously. His opponent ducked and dodged gracefully, almost like a dancer. She knew a man who moved like that, loved such a man. It couldn't be.

The intruder appeared to have his own knife out, and both seemed to be swiping air as the dance continued, until the bigger man's hand closed on El Gato's wrist and she heard the snap and saw the knife drop from the Apache chief's limp hand. El Gato's opponent flipped the Apache onto the ground like a rag doll, leaping on him and driving a knee into the Apache's groin, rendering El Gato helpless before he sheathed his own knife. She assumed now it was Oliver who clamped the sides of El Gato's head and began to hammer the skull against a protruding stone. The head must have been near mush when Oliver released it. But he was not finished. He eased the knife from its sheath again, pushed what remained of El Gato's head back and slowly ran the blade across the Apache's throat.

Tabitha had never seen the usually calm, patient Oliver Wolf explode in such a rage. She watched him silently with wide eyes as he got up and turned toward her, stepping across the gap between them, kneeling near her feet and slicing the ankle bonds. Then he moved along her side reached across her chest and cut the rawhide strip that held her wrist and repeated the cut with the other. He clutched her hand and got to his feet, pulling her up with him. He wrapped his arms about her, kissing the top of her head, and she collapsed into his embrace. She began sobbing uncontrollably, and Wolf just rubbed her back softly and allowed her to cry herself dry.

Finally, Tabitha began to regroup and pulled away. "How did you find us?"

"First, the gunfire brought me to Cal and the others. I helped them out some along the way, but you weren't there. If you hadn't screamed, I wouldn't have found you in time. I saw the bastard on top of you and just kept on running till I crashed into him and we both went flying."

"Cal . . . Delgado . . . Sunrise?"

"They're okay. Apaches are either dead or gone. I think we're finished with them here, but we've got another helping waiting to the north, I'm afraid. I brought a few extra horses, but we've got to figure out how to get Delgado to them."

Tabitha suddenly shivered and then remembered she was unclothed. "I'd better get dressed."

Wolf stepped back, pointing to garments that had been tossed haphazardly near the base of a tree by Delgado. "Need help?"

"No. I'm fine." Oliver had seen her naked more times than she could count, but somehow it was different now. She was carrying another man's child, and she had essentially run away from Oliver without explanation. She doubted they had a future together. It was all so complicated. There was so much to be sorted out, and she may have escaped from El Gato, but there were other Apaches chasing their scalps.

Chapter 34

WOLF RODE AHEAD with Tabby pressed against his back, arms wrapped about his waist and hands clasped over his belly. He savored her touch and nearness, although he sensed she had been a reluctant passenger. Since her initial embrace, she had been avoiding him, but he had taken charge and decided the riding arrangements. Cal was the sole rider of his own bay gelding, and Wolf had claimed a strong-looking sorrel gelding from the spare mounts to replace the injured Owl.

Wolf and Cal had carried Delgado, a smaller man, almost a mile to the gulch where Wolf had staked the mounts. Now the Navajo was saddled on his own mount with Sunrise astride behind him, balancing her husband as the horses loped over the flatter desert country. Delgado leaned forward in the saddle and had to be hurting, but he did not flinch or complain as they moved steadily to the rendezvous with their friends and the ransomed captives.

Wolf calculated sunrise was not more than an hour distant when they neared the stream and surrounding grove. There was no evidence of life there, but he could see orange spots on the horizon, he judged a mile distant, indicating fires there. The faint sounds of chanting and drums of war drifted their way. They were in luck for the moment. Evidently, El Gato's tribesmen did not share his penchant for the night and were stoking up their courage for a daylight battle.

They rode into the camp after a brief challenge by Fears Nothing, who vacated his station briefly after seeing that his parents were with Wolf, racing to his mother's side to help slide Delgado from the horse's saddle. Wolf intervened when he witnessed the struggle mother and son were having. They retrieved Delgado's bedroll and spread it out for the patient in some space stingily surrendered by the trees and undergrowth.

Wolf summoned North Star, the party's unofficial medic by virtue of his doctoring of Wolf's stallion. North Star examined Delgado and said, "Not so easy, but the lead must come out. I think I can do this but not until daylight and after we deal with the Apaches."

Wolf and Cal staked out the horses, and Wolf located Owl and checked the stallion's injury. He feathered his fingers over the area around the wound gently and did not detect undue swelling. He pressed his cheek to the horse's soft muzzle and praised him for his hard work and valiance, receiving a nicker of thanks in reply. Wolf had loved many horses, but this stallion that he had rescued from the slaughter of Comanche horses by the Army at Palo Duro Canyon held a special place in his heart.

He walked away from the horses, his eyes casting about for Tabby. He saw her near one of the crude fortifications talking with Jael and assumed she was recounting the story of their escape. He noticed that she carried her rifle and had the ammunition belt slung across her chest, ready to pitch into the fight when the time came. Her proficiency with a rifle would be welcome then.

He loved this woman in all the ways a man could love, and nothing could ever rip her from his soul. He had been so confident that she returned that kind of love, not only the intense physical attraction that can sometimes deceive and fade away, but the friendship, sharing, and trusting that nurtures a love that shrugs off life's storms and endures to the grave. But he had already steeled himself. He was an artist, by nature a dreamer, and perhaps he had not painted an accurate portrait of their relationship in his mind. Wolf had accepted he might never reach her again. All that mattered was that Tabby lived.

Wolf walked to the edge of the tangled grove and peered out onto the desert. A glowing orange sliver on the horizon warned that day's first light was only minutes away. He had thought attack at dawn was likely. "Get to your stations everybody. Tabby, you can stick with Jael. Cal, would you get with Fears Nothing? I'll be the swing man and go wherever more fire power is needed."

He saw dust rising from the Apache encampment. Mounting the horses, he concluded. The dust cloud began to roll toward the besieged defenders. "Hold your fire till I signal."

Wolf retrieved his own Winchester and waited. At first, it appeared they were coming head-on, but at the last second the mass split with part veering southerly and the others angling northerly. They apparently intended to circle the grove, seeking horses as he originally expected. This suited him fine. Spreading out would make it more difficult to concentrate their force at a single spot and overrun the defenders' circle with sheer numbers. As the Apaches edged nearer, Wolf yelled, "Fire at will."

The others started firing, but not recklessly he was pleased to note, steadily and methodically. Two Apaches tumbled from their horses, and another, evidently wounded, broke from the group and retreated, leaning forward against his mount's neck. He put their numbers at thirty-five, maybe a few more, certainly enough to overpower his group with the right strategy. A tall warrior raised a handless arm and signaled to the warriors before he headed away with the others falling in behind. He assumed that the leader was One Hand, the warrior who had claimed Sunrise for his wife and had joined El Gato at the trading negotiations.

Jael had told Wolf she thought they might face as many as sixty warriors based upon the tally she made while she was in the village. He hoped the lower number meant that some of the dissenters had declined to join the chase. He gathered the others to collect their thoughts, but he had already decided.

"They were just testing us," Wolf said. "Trying to locate our guns and determine how many. I think we surprised them some, because they wouldn't have any way of knowing we had reunited or that El Gato and most of his party are dead. We can hold out a long time if they keep circling and maybe wear them down if they do that. But I don't think we can count on that. If they look like they are going to hit one spot with a mass, I'd like Tabby and Cal to move to that area. I'll be there, too. The rest of you stay put in case smaller bunches peel off to hit us someplace else. We can't let them work in behind us. We have only one other choice."

"What's that?" Tabitha asked.

"Saddle up and make a run for it."

"We can't do that. Not with the shape Delgado's in. Besides, they are too many. We'd just make good targets. You know that. You're just trying to make us think this is a democracy. Right now, it's not. You're the general, self-appointed or not."

Same old Tabby, telling it just like she sees it and lacing her words with a hint of sarcasm. He thought he had seen a hint of a smile and the old sparkle in her eyes when she looked directly at him and spoke those words, though.

Wolf said, "We stay. Take your places."

It seemed like they had waited an hour, but Wolf supposed it had been more like fifteen minutes when the swirling dust started moving their way again. As he had feared and half-expected, this time only a small number of warriors peeled away from the main body. The others were headed like a bison herd in the direction of North Star's station. Wolf immediately moved in beside the Pueblo-Navajo and was quickly joined by Cal and Tabby. They clustered, allowing no more than a yard between shooters.

"Anytime," Wolf said, "they're plenty close." He fired off a shot but couldn't see he did any damage, but Tabby, positioned to his right, squeezed her Winchester's trigger, and a rider flew off his horse. He was not surprised. She was probably the best shot of the bunch.

But the Apaches were not easy targets. They slung down behind the sides of their horses, forcing the defenders to take down a mount to stop the rider, which Wolf flinched at. Some of the attackers were sliding or even leaping from their horses now, hitting the ground, rolling and jumping up to charge the grove, dodging, weaving and diving to the ground again. They were closing in, and Wolf called for a pull-back when the Apaches reached the trees. One warrior broke through the trees and leaped for Jael with war axe raised, but Cal slammed the Apache's head with his rifle butt and dropped him before the axe arced down. The warrior's tribesmen trailed but they were coming through the trees too fast. Soon it would be hand to hand, and he feared his crew of women, children and injured would be no match. He fired wildly, as did his comrades, levering cartridges into the rifle chambers until they were empty, but there was no time to reload.

Suddenly, there was more gunfire behind the oncoming Apaches, and the attackers turned and seemed to be confused as they saw their tribesmen falling, racing away afoot or on their horses. There was chaos and panic in their ranks, and the attackers wheeled, fleeing from the trees and joining the retreat. Wolf saw several felled when they emerged from the trees and got his first glimpse of their saviors.

Navajos, chasing down their Apache enemies with a vengeance. No quarter. The panic-driven devils were on the run. El Gato's band was being decimated, and it appeared the Navajo warriors were not finished with the chase. Then a familiar face appeared outside the grove, dismounted and tied his horse to a branch. Sundog ducked to dodge a low-hanging limb and came through the trees, a huge grin pasted on his face. The young man spoke something in Navajo, and Wolf looked at North Star for translation.

North Star said, "Sundog says he is glad we waited for them. They slept late this morning."

Chapter 35

TABITHA HAD SEEN Manuelito at the Diné village prior to the first Navajo search for captives taken in the raid. The Apaches routed, the Diné war party had joined the Wolf-led rescuers and escapees. Nearly twenty Navajo warriors had made the journey across the desert, motivated by a slim hope they might bring back the captives and exact revenge on the Apache killers and abductors. They had accomplished both admirably.

Manuelito had directed his warriors to set up camp. There was fresh water here and grass for the horses now that they could move the animals out of the trees to graze nearby. Lookouts would be posted near the remuda and at the edge of the camp, but there was little concern the Apaches would return, especially when there was no El Gato to spur them back.

Now Manuelito circulated casually among the former captives and their rescuers, spending considerable time kneeling next to Delgado while North Star, with Sundog's assistance, extracted the bullet fragments from the wounded Navajo's hip. The famed chief, who had led the Diné first in war and then to peace, with his stocky frame and kind face, did not conform to one's image of a fierce warrior, but he carried with him an aura, a presence that told an observer this was no ordinary man. His voice was soft, and his manner calm and unpretentious, but people listened when he spoke and stepped aside and followed when it was time for him to lead. She knew another man like that. Oliver Wolf.

As if reading her mind, Manuelito looked her way, his gentle eyes meeting hers. He rose to his feet and walked toward her, a reassuring smile on his face. By all appearances, he was an ordinary man, attired in cottons and a simple red band of cloth tied about his head. He wore no feathers or other insignia of rank or standing. When he reached her, he extended both hands and clasped her right hand between them. He held her hand between his two for some time, but they were not intrusive or unwelcome.

He did not speak until he released her hand. "You are free now. If you are Christian, El Gato burns in hell. It matters not. He cannot harm you."

She was not surprised at his precise English. A man who insisted his children attend the white man's schools and learn their language and ways would demand no less of himself. "Sometimes, the harm is never done." She did not understand why she told him this.

He nodded. "It can seem so." He touched chest and tapped softly. "But we have the power within ourselves to end it, to store the experience away as one of life's lessons and go on and find our happiness. We have choices. I am told you are a woman of thought and words. I think you are one of those who carries on a struggle between head and heart." He touched his head and then pressed his open hand to his chest. "I have endured this battle over my lifetime and have learned that sometimes the head should win, but there are others when it is best the heart gain victory. Your challenge is to sort these out. But I know you will, and when you do, El Gato's harm will be ended." He paused. "And you will step onto the trail that will lead you and your child to peace and happiness. I promise this, my friend."

Manuelito turned and walked away before she could reply. He had saved her a hesitant and clumsy response because her mood was not receptive to his words. But he knew about the baby that grew within her body. How could he? Jael knew, but her friend would have said nothing. She shivered at the thought of the chief's clairvoyance.

She slept most of the morning on top of an old buffalo robe that was Jael's bedroll when she traveled. Jael was curled up an arm's length away. Tabitha awakened when she heard excited voices and hurried activity in the camp. Jael was already up and looking to the east when Tabitha joined her. Dust, riders. Lots of them. Were the Apaches returning with reinforcements? Tabitha tensed but then noticed that the riders were moving slowly their way and, as they came into view, some were walking. Women and children, as well. This was not a war party.

Now, the group angled away from the ridge, heading west, but two riders separated from the travelers, one leading a horse, and moved in the camp's direction. Tabitha recognized them and took off at a run toward the approaching visitors. Jael followed a few paces behind.

When she neared the riders, the woman dismounted and raced toward her. "Ta-Bee," she yelled. "I know Ta-Bee be here."

The women embraced. Tabitha said, "What are you doing here?"

"Go San Carlos. Bring Ta-Bee horse." She turned back to Moon Watcher, who sat stoically astride his mount. He handed his wife the reins of the horse that stood next to his own. Walks Far led the black, white-footed gelding to Tabitha and placed the reins in her hand.

"Socks," Tabitha said. "I never expected to see him again. And saddled and ready to ride. I cannot thank you enough."

"More friend Tab-Bee." Walks Far stepped to the gelding's side and pointed to the rifle scabbard suspended from the saddle that had been Tabitha's.

Tabitha stepped near to see what her friend was pointing at. For an instant she was breathless when she saw it. She raised her hand, so her fingers could caress the rifle's stock. Her Henry.

She turned to Walks Far. "How did you get the rifle?"

Walks Far shrugged. "Go to wickiup. Take."

"I will never forget this. And I will not forget you. I will find you again at San Carlos, and I will locate members of your Diné clan. Someday you will see them again. Until then, my friend, I wish you a safe journey. Thank you." She hugged the Navajo-Apache woman and could not hold back the tears streaming down her cheeks. Only when she started to lead the gelding away did she notice that Jael, speaking Apache, had taken up a conversation with Moon Watcher.

When Jael caught up with her and the Apache couple had headed back to join the reservation-bound Apaches, Tabitha said, "May I ask what you and Moon Watcher were talking about?"

"I asked him if he knew that El Gato was dead. He said he had assumed as much since El Gato had not returned to the village. He was certain of it when he saw you were alive. If El Gato were alive, you would have been dead by now. He seemed relieved for the confirmation, though. He told me the Apaches who stayed behind plan to join Victorio. He thinks the Apache wars will continue for many months, perhaps, for several years yet. This was no more than a skirmish. But you didn't ask about this." She patted the saddlebags slung over her shoulder. "He gave me this."

"The ransom gold?"

"It appears to be."

"He's a good man. I hope he won't face punishment when he returns to San Carlos."

"I told him about our law firm and my representation of the tribes. I said I would try to help him and his band and that I would send a message to the agent at San Carlos with a letter for translation. I promised I could help his people deal with the government. I don't know if they will fare as well the Navajo and Comanche, though. They need advocates, but leaders like Manuelito and Quanah are even more important to their fate. Moon Watcher could be such a person, but I do not know the politics of power among the Apaches. And then there is the President and congress. God knows what they will decide to do with these people or how the bureaucrats will implement their policies. Good intentions aren't enough. Add a spoonful of ignorance and another of corruption, and you still end up with a lethal stew for the weak and unwary."

"My brother's cynicism must be contagious. I think you caught it."

"No. I had it long before I met and married Joshua Rivers."

Chapter 36

JAEL WAS SADDENED and perplexed by the coolness she had witnessed between Tabby and Oliver during the week's journey back to the village on the Navajo reservation. She also found herself angry at Tabby, who was clearly avoiding Oliver and putting the distance between them. She had already caused the man enough grief with her sudden, unannounced departure from Santa Fe, as far as Jael was concerned.

Jael and Oliver had been anxious to return to Santa Fe, and Jael had assumed Tabby would accompany them. No, Tabby had insisted she was going to return to the Navajo village and continue with the research for her book. She had already lived a novel, Jael figured. Wasn't that enough for now at least? Wolf and Jael had agreed they would join the trek to the village, stay a few days, and then head back home, with or without, Tabby.

The return to the village by the search party and the captives the previous day had triggered a night of celebration by the Hawk clan. Manuelito had ridden out shortly after sunrise with the other non-Hawk members of his party, and now, with high noon approaching, the village had quieted, and occupants were settling into routines.

Tabby had spent the night in Still Water's hogan, where she had apparently lodged before. Still Water had also followed up with treatment of Cal's and Delgado's wounds. Jael found the young woman delightful and fascinating, obviously someone who had earned the respect of her clan. Tabby and Still Water were walking somewhere now and had invited her to join them, but she had declined to join them on the pretext that she had to prepare for the next day's departure. In fact, she had decided to give Tabby free rein before she confronted her upon the pairs' return.

She had also turned down an invitation to share the hogan, choosing instead to spread her robe under the stars and bed down within a half dozen feet from Oliver last night. She supposed he would have been content enough without her presence, but she refused to isolate and abandon him after all that had happened.

She saw Oliver now, sitting with North Star and Cal in front of the vacated hogan the cousin had claimed, and which Cal shared temporarily. Oliver waved at her, signaling that she should join them.

When she neared, Cal said, "Sit yourself down, Jael. Some nice ladies have dropped more food off than we can eat in a week." The men held plates full of beans, beef slices and bread, and platters of a variety of breads and a pan of apple cobbler-type dessert rested on a mat within easy reach. She did not have to be asked twice. Wolf handed her a tin plate, spoon and two-tined fork, and she knelt and scooped into a pot of beans resting on coals inside the circle they had formed. Jael filled her plate with the other delights and sat down council-style with one leg tossed over the other, just like the men. Another reason she had always preferred britches.

She found herself suddenly ravenous and quickly adapted to the silence of folks who had not eaten a decent meal for days, focusing upon the happy task of devouring this unfamiliar abundance. After they turned to the dessert, Cal said, "I'll be riding out with you and Oliver tomorrow. I want to stop in Santa Fe and talk with Danna before I head up to the ranch to try to talk to Erin. I need some legal advice, and Little Sis said Danna's the lawyer to see about family fusses. Is that right?"

"Yes, she handles those cases for the firm."

"Well, I'm off the bottle for good. North Star here's convinced me I can't touch the fire water ever again. I'll see if Erin wants to have a try at patchin' things up. If she don't, the ranch came from her family, and I'll walk away from it. But I ain't walking away from those kids, and I'm going to make sure she knows it. If we can't work it out, I'll hire Danna to take it to a judge."

North Star said, "I am staying for a spell. I will have a letter for Cal to take to my mother after he leaves Santa Fe and passes through Taos on his way north."

Jael smiled, "This wouldn't have anything to do with a pretty lady named Still Water, would it?"

He grinned sheepishly. "It does. We haven't known each other long enough to be certain what might be. She will never leave the Diné. She says this is her destiny. Maybe it is mine, too. I can raise horses here and give my brother a chance to take over the ranch near Taos. Partner with him, maybe, and go back sometimes to check on things and visit my mother. And I don't think it would take much to get my mother to visit me and her folks here. She says she is Diné. Maybe she would just come home."

She would see the husband and family she loved soon. North Star and Cal had at least set tentative courses for their lives. Oliver remained silent. She knew he had hoped Tabby would be going back to Santa Fe with them and that the couple would just pick up where they left off before she departed those months back. It was not that simple for either Oliver or Tabby, and she did not feel free to explain just how complicated things really were. But Tabby was going to do it before this day was out.

"Oliver, I am going to speak to Tabby after we clean up things here. She will talk to you this afternoon. It's time."

Chapter 37

TABITHA AND STILL Water had enjoyed a quiet walk along the stream below the village. She appreciated that Still Water was a person who easily endured long silences and likely was satisfied to disappear into her own world until words were called for. As they moved back up the slope to the village, Tabitha finally asked her about what she had been thinking. "What if I would stay here? Is there a place for me among the Diné?"

Still Water seemed to ponder the question. "Do you mean make your home here?"

"Yes."

"You would be welcome here."

"I told you about the baby. Would a half-Apache child be accepted among the Diné?"

Still Water laughed. "Many Diné carry Apache blood. Just as many descend from Mexicans and, more recently, the whites. We are more a culture and way of life than a race. Yes, you and your child would be welcome here. I am glad you take pride in your Diné blood and accept it as a part of you. If you do not choose to live here, I hope you will make many visits to our homeland. There is much for you to learn and write about. But you are not Diné. Do you really want to live out your life here, or do you just wish to escape to our land? Hide from ghosts you are afraid to face? Think about this."

When they approached Still Water's hogan, Tabitha was surprised to find Jael standing outside, arms folded across her chest, eyes glaring daggers and teeth nibbling at her lower lip as she was wont to do when angered. Cal would have said she "had a burr up her ass."

"Are you upset about something, Jael?" Tabitha asked.

"We need to talk."

Still Water said, "I should visit Paloma. You may talk in my hogan."

Tabitha guessed Still Water had read Jael's pose as well and wanted no part of it.

Tabitha led Jael into the hogan, and they each sat down on one of Still Water's benches facing each other. "Something's troubling you," Tabitha said. "Tell me."

"You are troubling me. I'm disgusted with the way you are treating Oliver. This is not the Tabby I have known for almost four years now. You ran out on him and didn't even have the decency to face him and explain where you were going or why. He wouldn't have tried to stop you."

"No, but he would have wanted to come with me."

"Oh, you poor soul. Plagued with a man who wants to be with you."

"I didn't want to interrupt his work, his life."

"Did it ever occur to you that his life was so much less without you? Still is?"

"I don't know that."

"And he drops everything and rides across New Mexico Territory to take on the Apaches the instant he hears you are in trouble. Merely risks his life and saves yours? And now you avoid him, barely speak to him. I'm disgusted with your behavior. I don't know you."

Tabitha stammered, "It . . . it's the baby. I'm humiliated. Being pregnant changes everything."

"Do you mean you no longer love Oliver? I know you did. You agonized when he asked you to marry him, thought you would eventually."

"I do love him. More than ever. I just cannot bring myself to hurt him more."

"You can't hurt him more than the torture you are inflicting on him now. He doesn't understand your behavior, your distance. You will never be loved more by another man, and still you treat him like this. Quit your damn whining. It's unbecoming. Sickening. The least you can do is talk to him. Tell him about the baby. If you won't be with him, have the decency to tell him why. Are you afraid he will scream at you? Hit you?"

"Of course not. He's incapable of doing either."

"Talk to him."

Tabitha knew she had to face this. "I will. Can you find him for me?"

"He is waiting at North Star's wickiup. I will send him here."

Shortly, Oliver Wolf ducked through the wickiup opening. Tabitha remained seated and looked up at him, tendering a nervous smile and then nodding at the bench Jael had vacated. He sat down and looked at her, his face stoic, as usual. But she could read the curiosity in his eyes.

"Did Jael tell you what this is about?"

He surrendered a small smile. "Only that we are going to talk."

"I don't know where to start. At the beginning, I guess. I was a coward and dishonest. I should have talked to you. I never should have left like that. I'm sorry. Terribly sorry. I hope someday you will be able to forgive."

"I already have."

She sighed. "You came for me. You saved my life. And I don't think I ever even thanked you for that."

"Not necessary."

"Thank you. I have been a total bitch."

"Never."

"I have to tell you something. It's very difficult. It doesn't excuse my recent behavior. But maybe it will help you understand." She took a deep breath. "I'm pregnant." She saw him brighten, and she quickly continued, "By El Gato. I am carrying the child of the man you killed."

She saw only sadness in his eyes. His silence told her nothing.

"I intend to carry this child and raise him or her. Otherwise, I don't know where this takes my life. I am living in limbo."

Wolf said, "Think about this. Don't answer me now. I love you, Tabby. I want to spend my life with you. I asked you once to marry me. I am asking you again. Marry me, and we will make your child ours."

"You could love a child fathered by that man?"

"That man was a great warrior. In another time he might have been a statesman or leader for peace. He was a man of this time and this place. We are all captives of our experience."

"But what would we tell this child? The truth? That his or her father was Apache? That you killed his father?"

"We would decide when the time came years from now. Perhaps just some of the truth. Silence is not necessarily a lie. Truth serving as a sword is not always noble. There will likely be more serious challenges before that time, but they would be easier if we faced them together."

"You make it sound so simple," Tabitha said.

"The questions you must answer are these: Do you love me? Do you want to make your life with me? You and your child? Don't answer now. Stay with your Navajo friends so long as you must to sort this out. You know where to find me. You know where you will be loved. You and our child."

Wolf stood to leave but first held out his arms in an invitation. She got up and fell into his embrace, clinging tightly to him before he stepped back and slipped out into the sunlight.

She would have answered if Oliver had stayed a few minutes longer. She remembered Manuelito's words about choosing between heart and head. On occasion, you did not have to choose. Heart and head led you the same way.

The next morning, Tabitha saddled Smokey and tied Socks, purchased from Still Water, to a lead rope. She mounted the gelding and reined in beside Oliver, reached over and took his hand. "I love you," she said. "And the answer is 'yes.'"

About the Author

Ron Schwab is the author of the popular Western series, The Law Wranglers, The Coyote Saga, and The Lockes, as well as several standalone novels, including Grit, a winner of the Western Fictioneers Peacemaker Award for Best Western Novel. He is a member of the Western Writers of America, Western Fictioneers, and Mystery Writers of America.

Ron's earlier published works included the suspense novels, Crocodile Fears and The Buddy System, both printed under a pseudonym, Michael J. Stewart. He is a member of the Western Writers of America, Western Fictioneers, and Mystery Writers of America.

Ron and his wife, Bev, divide their time between their home in Fairbury, Nebraska and their cabin in the Kansas Flint Hills.

Made in United States
Troutdale, OR
07/20/2023

11448027R00202